# Praise for Gail Gaymer Martin:

"Gail Gaymer Martin's best book to date.
Real conflict and very likeable characters
enhance this wonderful romantic story."
—*Romantic Times* on
**LOVING HEARTS**

"Perhaps Gail Gaymer Martin's best, a
romantic suspense novel you'll want to read—
during the day!"
—*Romantic Times* on
**A LOVE FOR SAFEKEEPING**

"Gail Gaymer Martin writes with compassion
and understanding…."
—*Romantic Times* on
**SECRETS OF THE HEART**

"…an emotional, skillfully written story
about mature subject matter. You'll probably
need a box of tissues for this one."
—*Romantic Times* on
**UPON A MIDNIGHT CLEAR**

## Books by Gail Gaymer Martin

### Love Inspired

*Upon a Midnight Clear* #117
*Secrets of the Heart* #147
*A Love for Safekeeping* #161
*Loving Treasures* #177
*Loving Hearts* #199
*Easter Blessings* #202
  "The Butterfly Garden"
*The Harvest* #223
  "All Good Gifts"
*Loving Ways* #231

### Silhouette Romance

*Her Secret Longing* #1545
*Let's Pretend...* #1604

## *GAIL GAYMER MARTIN*

lives with her real-life hero in Lathrup Village, Michigan. After years of writing poetry, skits and church programs, Gail found her dream—writing novels. Gail is multipublished in nonfiction and fiction with sixteen novels and five novellas, and many more to come. Her Steeple Hill Love Inspired romance *Upon a Midnight Clear* won a Holt Medallion in 2001 and *A Love For Safekeeping* won the ACRW 2002 Book of the Year Award in short contemporary and was nominated for Best Love Inspired Novel of 2002 by *Romantic Times*.

Besides writing, Gail enjoys traveling, singing, guest-speaking and presenting workshops for writers. She believes that God's gift of humor gets her through even the darkest moments and she is awed by the Lord's continued blessings.

She loves to hear from her readers. Write to her on the Internet at gail@gailmartin.com or at P.O. Box 760063, Lathrup Village, MI, 48076, and visit her Web site at www.gailmartin.com.

# LOVING WAYS

## GAIL GAYMER MARTIN

Published by Steeple Hill Books™

STEEPLE HILL BOOKS

Steeple
Hill™

ISBN 0-373-87241-0

LOVING WAYS

Visit us at www.steeplehill.com

**Printed in U.S.A.**

We have renounced secret and shameful ways;
we do not use deception, nor do we distort the word
of God. On the contrary, by setting forth the truth
plainly we commend ourselves to every man's
conscience in the sight of God.
—*2 Corinthians* 4:2

In memory of my mom, Nellie Riley,
whose love and support will never be forgotten.
This is the first novel I've written that she hasn't
read. I pray God has a library in heaven.

# Chapter One

"Dear Lord! Help!"

Ken Dewitt stopped in his tracks as the piercing cry shot through the screen door. He dropped the edger on the sidewalk and bolted up the porch stairs.

"Annie! What is it?" he called through the screen.

Muffled sounds came from within the house.

"Where are you?" Ken called again. Then without concern for manners, he flung open the door and followed her cries for help to the second floor. Hearing the fear in Annie's voice sent memories pounding through him with each thump of his footsteps on the staircase.

Dashing down the hallway, Ken looked through the open doorways until he spotted Annie O'Keefe's slender form crouching over a body lying on the floor beside a hospital bed.

"Pa," she called, her voice quaking.

His lungs knotted as he hurried to her side. "What happened?"

She struggled for control and rose, shaking her head, her arms flailing with confusion, tears rimming her eyes. "I don't know, but I think he's breathing."

Enveloped in the odor of medicine and illness, Ken squatted, feeling for the older man's pulse. His two fingers slid along the wrist until he detected a steady beat. "He's alive."

At Ken's words, the man's wrinkled face grimaced and his pale-grey eyes fluttered open. "Who are you?"

"Your landscaper, Mr. O'Keefe. Ken Dewitt."

Annie hovered above him, her fair skin even paler with concern. "You're okay, Pa."

The older man's face twisted as if sorting out their words. Then his eyes narrowed, and he frowned as if he'd found himself in some kind of irritating situation.

"You fell out of bed…it seems," Ken said.

A faint harumph rattled from the older man's throat. "You're no doctor, are you?" His dazed eyes shifted from side to side until he spotted Annie. "What happened, girl?"

She released a sigh and knelt beside Ken. A whiff of sweet fragrance washed over him. "I don't know, Pa. I think you fell out of bed like he said." She brushed her trembling fingers across her father's creased forehead.

"I didn't fall," Roy O'Keefe said, his voice stronger. "I tried to get up. I need to use the bathroom."

Annie shot up, propping her fists against her trim hips. "You're not to get up alone. You know that." She shook her head and gave Ken a hopeful look. "Can you—?"

"Let me handle this," Ken said, shifting around to brace the man's shoulders and help him to a sitting position. Ken eyed the man from behind. "You have a knot on your head, sir."

The older man jerked his arms sideways, whacking Ken's shin with a sharp elbow, and felt the lump.

Pain rolled up Ken's leg as memory took him back years earlier to his father's wallops across Ken's ears. Slamming the door of his past, he stepped aside while Annie inspected the lump with her fingertips.

"Looks like you might have knocked yourself out for a minute," she said while her gray eyes searched Ken's in question.

Her father cringed and gave her a glowering look. "I don't remember nuthin'."

"I'm calling an ambulance, Pa," Annie said. She gave Ken a knowing look, as if she were prepared for her father's response.

"Oh no you won't." He wriggled from her grasp.

Annie shrugged. "This is my life."

Ken eyed her father, still feeling the throb in his shin. The duffer might be weak, but he wielded a mighty strong elbow. "Let me get behind you, Mr. O'Keefe, and I can help you up."

Annie's father stopped fighting and allowed Ken to boost him upward into a standing position while Annie waited.

When he'd balanced himself, the older man rested his arm on his daughter's shoulders. "Now…can I go to the bathroom or should I go right—"

"Pa, don't be silly."

His muscles tied with frustration, Ken looked at Annie, as pretty as a flower, and sensed the daily stress she endured, just as his mother had done for so many years. Death had been a gift to her mother. But Annie didn't give in to her father's tirade. Ken saw her straighten her back ready for a fight.

"Let me," Ken said, moving in place and bracing the man's unsteady weight through the doorway to the bathroom across the hall. Once Ken settled him inside, he backed out and pulled the door closed to give him privacy.

"I'm so sorry," Annie said, resting her back against the doorjamb across the hallway, her fair complexion flushed now with seeming exasperation, her otherwise pleasing face lined with years of stress. She ran her hand along the nape of her neck beneath a knot of hair and looked at him with tired eyes.

At first, Ken passed it off with a shrug, yet he felt nudged by a rising desire to put his arm around her to offer some support. He withdrew from his thoughts and cleared his throat. "Glad I could help."

She nodded a thankyou. "I've told him so many times to let me know when he needs the bedpan." Annie shifted her hand from the back of her neck and rubbed her fingertips along her temple where small lines crinkled around her eyes. "It's frustrating. I'm not as young as I used to be. I can't support his weight unless he's having a good day."

Ken thought about her father's "good" elbow, but kept the joke to himself. Without help, how could she give her father the care he needed? Annie's problem had become his own since he'd felt drawn to her. He'd been fighting the feeling for months.

"You might want to find a place…" Looking at her strained expression, he stopped and switched direction. "You might want to…give me a call if you need help. You have my phone number." Hearing his offer startled him.

Annie's tension seemed to melt, and her expression softened. "You're our landscaper, not a doctor…but thanks."

"I mean it, Annie. Call me." Ken listened to his words echoing in his head and wished he hadn't become so helpful. Almost sappy.

The toilet flushed, and Ken waited a moment, then tapped on the door before pushing it open. The man clung to the basin, rinsing his hands under the tap. The familiar scent of soap filled the air.

"Thanks," the old man mumbled, his voice gentler.

"You're welcome, sir," Ken said as he bolstered the man against his side and aided him back into bed. *Sir* seemed the only touch of dignity he could offer him

Her face set in a frown, Annie watched from the side, adjusting the bed sheet and smoothing the blanket.

Ken stepped backward, gave her a nod, then turned and passed through the doorway. He'd leave Annie and her father alone. As the elderly man had pointed out, Ken was no doctor. He wasn't even family.

Before he reached the bottom of the stairs, Annie called his name. He turned and looked toward her.

She moved down the staircase. Her platinum hair had been caught back in a clip and wisps had escaped to nestle against her rounded, flushed cheek. When she reached his side, he longed to brush the strands into place.

"What can I do to thank you?" Annie asked.

A strange sensation rolled through Ken's chest. He shook his head, surprised by the thoughts that filled him. He had no answer and continued down the stairs.

She followed, and at the bottom, she stepped past him, leaving her familiar flowery-scented trail. When she turned, the muscles in her face had relaxed and her lips curved into a meager smile. "Want to sit a minute?"

"Maybe later, Annie." Needing to escape, he grasped the screen-door handle and offered the first excuse he could think of. "I left my equipment outside. Someone could walk off with it."

"Oh. Yes," she said.

Ken sensed disappointment in her eyes. Why couldn't he relax and take time to talk with her? They'd done that many times when he'd found her sitting on the porch. It was as if she waited for him when he showed up to look after the trees and shrubs. Sometimes he'd stopped for himself. Just for someone to talk with. He liked her…but he couldn't get involved, even though his heart didn't want to agree.

He pushed open the door and eyed his gear still sitting where he'd left it. Taking two steps at a time off the porch, Ken reached the ground, and when he glanced over his shoulder, Annie watched him from behind the screen. Her loneliness made him ache.

Annie studied Ken a moment before turning back inside. After she stepped away from the sunlight, the gloom inside the house stifled her spirit. When she could, Annie liked to be outside when Ken arrived so they had a chance to talk. If she were honest, visiting with him often seemed the best part of her week.

The hedge trimmer sparked to life and its buzz droned into the house. As Annie made her way to the kitchen, the sound seemed to follow her, and she looked out the back window to see Ken striding along the yard's edge, his corded arms flexing as he guided the trimmer along the shrubs.

In Michigan's glaring May sun, Ken's strong jaw was darkened by a five o'clock haze that gave him a rugged look. The deep cleft in his chin appeared as a shadow below his firmly set mouth. Through the window, Annie noticed perspiration beading his face and splotching his blue T-shirt. Since the first day she'd hired him, Annie had found him appealing in a brooding way.

Feeling like a peeping Tom, she straightened the curtain and moved to the refrigerator. She opened the door and pulled out the lemonade container, partially filled, then opened the freezer and drew out a can of concentrate. She would top off the pitcher just in case Ken wanted something to drink when he finished.

Emotion knotted in her throat. A mature woman shouldn't grapple for conversation or friendship, but caring for her father had taken a bite out of her social life.

Social life? Who needed it?

She hated feeling sorry for herself. Besides having little choice, she *wanted* to take care of her father. One of his children should…and she was the only single one of the bunch. Annie had long given up on the idea of marriage. Who'd want to marry a forty-two-year-old woman tied to her father's illness? She hated that issue, too, and dismissed it as self-pity.

The trimmer silenced, and Annie waited, not wanting to look like an over-anxious teenager. She monitored her eagerness until she felt certain Ken had reached the front. She took a deep breath before ambling toward the front door.

Ken stood behind the truck, loading his equipment into the bed. He mopped the perspiration from his brow with a handkerchief, then shoved it into his back pocket before returning up the sidewalk toward the pruning debris. His gaze swept the shrubs as if making a final inspection.

Overpowering the urge to dart onto the porch, Annie inched open the screen and leaned against the frame.

Ken's gaze lifted, and he gave her a nod. ''Does your offer still hold?''

Pleasure settled over her. She hadn't wanted to ask

again and hear another refusal. "Sure. Come in when you're finished. I made some lemonade."

He nodded and went about his business.

Annie returned to the kitchen and filled two tumblers with ice, then added the liquid. She had baked oatmeal cookies that morning, so she filled a plate then set it on the table. She rested against the counter to wait.

A few minutes later, she heard a rap on the door followed by the screen door's faint squeak.

"In the kitchen," she called. When she heard his footsteps in the hall, Annie swept away the hair from her cheeks. Ken came into sight, and she smiled, motioning toward the table.

He sauntered in, wiping his hands on his jeans.

"You can wash up if you'd like." She pointed toward the small half bath off the back entry.

He followed the direction of her hand with a nod.

She watched him stride across the room, the scent of sun and cedar filling her senses. Amazed at her exhilaration, Annie lifted her tumbler and pressed the icy glass against her cheek. Again, her confidence took flight along with her social life. Ken had filled her dreams too often, and she had to remember the fantasy was hers, not his. She'd so often sensed his reserve.

In a moment, she heard his footsteps and sank into the chair as he returned. "Here you go," she said, sliding the lemonade across the table toward him.

"Thanks." A soapy fragrance followed him to the

table. He lifted the glass and took a long drink. "Hits the spot."

Ken's brooding image touched Annie's senses like autumn foliage and the hazy smoke of a bonfire—as natural as the jeans and plaid shirts he wore. She admired his lean, sinewy build and his craggy features framed by graying brown hair. Ken was rough edges waiting to be smoothed by loving hands.

He'd nearly downed the liquid in one gulp, and Annie rose and brought the pitcher from the refrigerator. She filled his glass and set the container on the table.

"Guess I was thirsty." His gaze captured hers while he took another sip. When he finished, he settled into a chair. The craggy creases in his face hinted of some unknown deep emotion—hurt, betrayal, something that roused her curiosity.

Though they'd often talked on the porch, Annie felt awkward sitting beside him at the kitchen table. She rarely had anyone there now that her father couldn't maneuver the stairs. Once in a while, Sissy or Abby Hartmann, her next-door neighbors, would drop by for a moment. A couple weeks ago Sissy had stayed for a cup of tea. They'd sat and talked, but usually she sat at the table alone.

Annie focused on Ken's strong hands, his sturdy fingers wrapped around the cold glass. The silence settled over her and she pulled her attention upward. "Have a cookie. They're homemade."

His gaze left hers and traveled to the plate. "Oatmeal?"

She nodded. "You don't like them?"

"My favorite." He took one and sank his teeth into the soft cookie. "Thanks."

She nodded and watched him take another bite, his gaze directed to the distance.

"Living like this can't be easy," he said, motioning the cookie toward the second-floor. "Don't you have any family who can help you?"

She felt her back stiffen. He wasn't meddling, she realized. The doctor had asked her the same question, but she didn't have anyone willing…and *willing* was the key.

"My brothers and sisters live out of town. They have families so it's only right that I stay with Pa." She fidgeted with her tumbler, watching the condensation rings form on the table with each turn.

When she focused on him, a frown had settled on his face. She studied him, her curiosity urging her to ask what he had on his mind. Then she didn't have to ask.

He swallowed the last bite. "Seems you could use help." Ken brushed the napkin over his hands, then crumpled it and dropped it onto the table. "You know there's a nursing home not too far away and—"

Her fingers slipped from the glass to the table. "I couldn't do that. It's just not in me to…"

Ken's hand darted forward and caught her arm as if trying to stop her comment. "Look. It's none of my business. You do what you have to do."

Gloom weighed his expression, and she realized he'd meant to be kind.

She managed a pleasant look. "I appreciate your concern."

Ken flexed his wrist and eyed his watch. "I'd better get going." He took a final swig of the drink and rose.

Annie watched him step forward as if he might touch her, but instead, he shifted away. Confusion filled his face as he jutted his hand toward her.

She peered at it a moment before realizing he was offering a handshake. She grasped his palm, feeling the warmth of his touch. "Thanks again for your help."

"Anytime." He paused a moment before turning.

Annie stood in place and watched him vanish through the doorway, taking the sunshine with him.

Ken pulled the rope on the chain saw, finding pleasure in the roar of the motor. He wished the sound could drown out the feelings that rumbled through him. All day while he moved from location to location, he'd pictured Annie standing above her father. The image flashed in his mind like flickering neon.

She'd looked helpless. Not small—though she was slender, Annie was five foot six or seven, he figured— but like someone caught in a trap. A lonely trap. The kind of loneliness Ken knew.

Ken bent down to toss a limb onto a pile, then clung to the pulsating handles and wished he could shake the feelings mounting in his gut.

Maybe he cared about Annie because in her he saw his mother, a woman so controlled by her environment she let her life fly past without even tasting it. Maybe he cared because…

No. He stopped that line of thinking. A woman like Annie needed a good wholesome man. A solid Christian. Not someone like him. Not with his background…his past. If Annie knew, she'd not only refuse him entrance into her house, but send him packing and find a new landscaper.

At times, Ken longed for companionship. He longed for life to be different, and so did Annie—he saw it in her eyes—but he couldn't fulfill her happiness. He could only wish. Pray is what some Christian's did. They asked God Almighty to forgive them and allow them to accept their due. But he wondered why. God punished sinners. He'd learned that as a child.

Turning off the saw, Ken stood a moment to gather his wits. This was his last job for the day, and he figured he wouldn't rest until he knew Annie had survived the stressful afternoon. The desire to check on her struck an alien chord. He'd been a loner so much of his life.

Still, with renewed energy, Ken let a plan settle into his thoughts and finished the trimming, then packed the equipment into the truck and drove to his bungalow. He showered and changed into a knit shirt, then grabbed a bite to eat while he reviewed his purpose. Finally, he climbed into his car and headed toward Washington Avenue.

Ken spotted Annie sitting on the porch as he neared her house. When he pulled into the drive and stepped from the car, her gray eyes widened until recognition settled on her face. "I didn't realize it was you at first."

"Why?" He slammed the car door.

"The car. You usually drive a truck."

"Right," he said, his attention drawn to her smoky gray eyes like misty haze.

Annie added a smile to her surprised expression. "What are you doing here?"

Ken ambled up the sidewalk asking himself the same question. "I dropped by to see how your father's doing." He grabbed the stair railing and took the steps two at a time, stopping at the porch edge and feeling out of place.

Annie sat on a porch swing with her legs stretched along the wooden seat. Her ankles peeked from beneath the hem of her beige slacks. She wore a pale purple sleeveless top the color of new lilacs. Her lipstick had faded leaving her mouth a natural pink.

"My father's fine," she said, closing the cover of the book she held. She tucked it beside her and slid her legs over the edge of the swing to the porch floor. "It's nice you stopped by."

Taking a single step to the right, Ken dug his hands into his pockets and rocked on his heels, wondering if she'd invite him to sit. He eyed the empty seat. "No concussion?"

"He seems okay."

"Glad to hear it." Ken shifted his feet, thinking he was a fool to stand there. He should give up or be more direct and say he'd come to visit with her.

Her troubled expression brightened and she chuckled. "Sorry, Ken. I should've invited you to sit. You'd think I'd lost my manners." She motioned to the wicker love seat. "That is if you have time."

He pulled his hands from his pockets. "I have time," he said, sinking into the cushion. "I can't think of anything better."

Her eyes narrowed as if pondering his statement. "Better? Than what?"

"You," he said.

"Me?" Her eyes widened and a tinge of color brightened her cheeks.

Ken rubbed the bridge of his nose, feeling nervous and out of his element. He hadn't come on to a woman in years, and he shouldn't be doing it now. "I can't think of anything better than being here with you."

# Chapter Two

Annie let Ken's words wash over her. *I can't think of anything better than being here with you.* She took a deep breath, wondering what he meant. She liked Ken. A lot. But she couldn't imagine a man as good-looking and wonderful as he was being interested in her. What did she have to offer anyone? She'd had lots of letdowns in her life. She didn't need another.

Ken leaned back against the wicker and rested his folded hands on his trim middle.

For the first time with him, Annie felt tongue-tied.

A breeze had picked up, cooling the hot afternoon air and lowering the humidity to something more bearable. Annie eased against the porch swing and curled her legs beneath her. As she rocked, the chain links gave a soft *squeak-squeak.* "I need to oil this thing one day."

Ken straightened and eyed the chain. "Next time I drop by in the truck, I'll take care of it."

"Thanks. You've already done too much for us."

"Why do you say that, Annie?" A deep frown creased his tanned forehead, and a disappointed look filled his eyes. "You're the one who's done too much."

She bit her lip, wanting so badly to open her heart to someone. She knew what God expected of her, and she tried hard not to give way to frustration. Right now, she was failing.

Ken leaned closer and rested his hand against her arm. "I didn't mean to upset you. I only wanted—"

"You didn't upset me." Annie felt the warmth of his hand rushing along her skin and addling her thoughts. She waited a moment before she could make eye contact. "I upset myself."

His mouth opened, then closed again as if he wanted to speak but didn't know what to say. He rested his arms on his knees, staring at the porch planks.

Only traffic noise broke the silence.

When he lifted his head, she saw concern in his eyes. "I don't understand how you could be upset with yourself."

"Maybe it's not upset. I suppose I'm angry…or disappointed or I…I don't know. I just don't like myself sometimes."

Ken leaned against the cushion while a dark shadow filled his face. "That makes no sense from where I'm sitting."

She searched his eyes, her mind sorting her

thoughts, wishing she could explain. "I'm forty-two. Too old to be dreaming."

"Yoo hoo!"

Annie straightened her back and looked next door over the porch wall. Her elderly neighbor, Sissy Hartmann, was standing on the porch of the rooming house she owned with her sister. She waved with a honeyed grin. Annie knew why. "Hello, Sissy. How are things at Loving Arms?"

"Wonderful, thank you, and better since it's finally cooling off," the elderly woman called. "Nice you can enjoy your company on the front porch." The words *your company* had an extra ring to them.

"It is," Annie said, then relaxed her back to break eye contact with her neighbor. Though thoughtful, the two sisters had little to do but watch the neighborhood's goings-on.

"Is that you, Ken Dewitt?" Sissy asked.

Ken grinned and stood, giving the woman a wave. "It's me, Miss Hartmann. Just checking on Annie's father. He had a fall today."

"Oh my. No," Sissy said, her voice filled with concern. "Is he all right now?"

"Yes. Just needs to get his strength back," Annie said, stretching her neck upward to see her neighbor.

"I'll make him some homemade chicken soup tomorrow, dear, and he'll be good as new," Sissy called.

"Thank you." Annie scrunched her head into her neck and eyed Ken with a grin. She waited for a moment until she heard the screen door close next door. "I should be ashamed of myself. They're so sweet."

"But so nosy."

Ken's rare smile made her chuckle. He was right. Nothing got past the two sisters. Still, their nearness helped Annie feel more secure.

Ken sat again and rubbed his craggy jaw. "I'm still curious. Tell me why you feel upset with yourself."

Feeling captured, Annie sat a moment, then shrugged. "Sometimes I'm frustrated. I hate self-pity."

"Frustrated? Because you feel stuck here?"

"I…I want to be here. Please don't think I don't. Like you said, I have options, but…"

"But you feel like you'd let down your father if you found help?" His look reflected an element of disbelief.

She nodded. "Yes, the heavenly Father."

His eyes narrowed as his frown deepened. "You mean you feel like you're letting down God?"

His gaze riveted to hers and made her uncomfortable.

"But Annie, if God's so almighty, He'd fix things. Look at it this way. You have options. A nursing home isn't the only choice. You could hire a…helper, or if your father's not doing…if he's near…." His face charged with discomfort. "There's always hospice. I don't know why we…why people create their own prisons. You need a break. You need a life of your own."

*You need a life of your own.* She had often thought

the same thing. She'd had a life once, but now Annie didn't know how to get a new life or how to use the one she had. "It's a long story and hard to put into words."

"Try me."

Her face washed with sadness, and Ken longed to erase what he'd said and let her live with her silent grief or hurt, but it was too late.

"You've met my father." Her direct gaze captured his. "He can be a handful, but through the years, he's softened." She looked away. "Since my mother died. It's like she'd been the center of his world. A crazy, volatile world, at times, but she stuck by him.

"You know," she said, "I think he realized for the first time that my mother was the only one who'd stuck by him through everything."

"And you did," Ken said.

She shook her head. "Not me. I'd moved to my own place…just like my brothers and sisters did."

Ken didn't know what to say. He wondered how she could forget that now and spend her life caring for a father who'd been a poor role model. The words struck Ken. What kind of a role model would he be for his children if he had any?

"I hated his drinking," Annie said, "and Pa's anger when he was under the influence. It's as if the bottle opened demons inside him."

Ken watched stress build on her face. Why had he pushed her on the subject? He knew better. "No sense in talking about it now, I suppose."

She shook her head. "No…it's good for me to talk.

It helps me remember why I came back home to live. I realized in the past years, when my father wasn't drinking, we knew he loved us. It wasn't him. It was the drink that ruined our lives.'' The swing gave a creak as she rose. ''God never fails us, Ken.''

She moved to the porch railing and looked out toward the lawn. ''And I guess, I didn't want to fail the Lord.'' She turned to face him. ''*Honor your father and mother,* God said, and I decided to do that. When my mom became ill I came home. Like I said, my dad changed. He seemed lost. Sure he kept his grumpy demeanor, but he softened. I couldn't abandon him after Mom died. He wasn't well, and I was the only one of the kids unmarried and still in Loving. I got used to it.''

Ken couldn't speak. He had no words that could capture his feelings. Annie's faith was strong. So strong he couldn't understand it.

Rather than abandon her parent when her four siblings had moved away, Annie stayed. She stuck to her duty…and her faith like gum to a shoe. Looking at it his way, Ken thought Annie had been abandoned by God just as he'd been.

''And you know what?'' Annie said. ''Despite my complaining about being Pa's nursemaid, despite the memories that drag me down sometimes, I'm going to miss him. I know. I see my father's life ebbing away, and I can't do a thing about it.''

As her eyes misted, a lump formed in Ken's chest. He was the one who'd prodded her to talk and now he felt helpless. Tears trickled down Annie's cheeks, and she lowered her head. Without thinking, Ken rose and brushed the tears from her eyes, then sat beside her on the swing.

"You've done all you could, Annie. You've been a good daughter."

She leaned into him, and he took her in his arms. She rested her head on his shoulder and Ken's heart filled with longing…a deep desire to make her smile. To give her happiness.

"Who's to say your father doesn't have years yet to live. He's a spunky guy." His thoughts shot back to earlier that day when her father whacked him in the shin. "So if he's still full of life, you should be, too."

She lifted her head and gazed at him as if in thought.

"Do you ever get out, Annie? To dinner or shopping…for yourself? Have you seen a movie on a big screen lately or walked along Lake Michigan on a spring day?"

She shifted her gaze to the lawn. "I've had responsibilities."

"But do you ever get out to enjoy yourself?"

Her eyes dimmed. "Not lately, but—"

"Time you did."

"The Hartmanns sit while I grocery shop," she said, "and I've had offers from church members. The other day one of the women volunteered to sit with Pa while I went out for my birthday."

Her birthday. His own birthday whisked through his thoughts. Birthdays came and went like Mondays.

One day no different from another. But Annie? How long had it been since anyone had stood around the table to sing Happy Birthday to her while she blew out her candles. The image sat in his thoughts like a bubble. "Did you take the lady up on her offer?"

"For my birthday, you mean?"

He felt disheartened by the discomfort in her eyes. He nodded.

"It's not until next week."

"Next week." A mission came to him. "Listen, Annie O'Keefe. You tell that church lady you'd like her to stay with your father, because you have plans for your birthday."

As fast as his spirit lifted, it took a nosedive. Why was he doing this? He'd already come on to her with his "I can't think of anything better than being with you" line, and he'd meant it. But anything he said was only empty promises. He would open his arms to Annie and then have to close them again. The horrid situation when he lived in Fremont knifed through him. What did he have to offer this woman? Nothing but trouble and more hurt for himself.

"Me?" The edges of her mouth curled as she watched his face. "I have plans? I don't think so."

"Yes you do." He'd set up the invitation and he'd follow through. "With me."

She arched an eyebrow as if wondering whether he was teasing. "Thanks, but I'm a big girl. I've lived for many years without a birthday party." A quiet chuckle left her. "No...I couldn't."

"Why not?"

"I don't like pity."

He ignored the comment. It wasn't pity. Far from it. She just deserved someone better than him. "Tell me the day and I'll tell you the hour."

She tilted her head, a questioning look in her eyes. "May twenty-ninth. Next Thursday."

"How about seven o'clock?"

"Seven?"

Ken locked wisdom in a corner of his mind and opened his heart. "Seven sharp."

Her joyful look sent his stomach on a carnival ride.

Annie opened the door and pushed back the screen as Sissy arrived with the promised chicken soup. Annie guessed more than the soup brought the gray-haired woman to her door. She wanted the scoop on Ken's after-work visit.

"Thanks. You're a good neighbor," Annie said, steering the woman to the kitchen and breathing in the rich scent of Sissy's offering.

"*Love your neighbor as yourself,*" Sissy said. "It's God's rule."

Annie knew it was God's rule. *Love your neighbor as yourself. Clothe yourselves with compassion, kindness, humility, gentleness and patience.* But she didn't remember a Bible verse about enjoying her own life.

"God's rule or not, I appreciate it," Annie said. "And it smells delicious."

"There's enough here for you both." Sissy set the pot on the stove burner, then turned away from the stove and folded her hands at her waist as if waiting for an invitation to sit.

"Would you like a cup of tea?" Annie asked, knowing her answer.

"That would be nice, dear."

Annie snapped on the burner beneath the teakettle while Sissy settled at the table.

"I was glad to see you had company," Sissy said. "You spend too much time alone."

Annie heard the comment and wondered which was the lesser evil in which to respond—her time alone or Ken's visit. "*Honor your father and mother,*" she murmured, thinking Sissy couldn't fault that statement.

"I know it's not my business, but your parents have lived beside Abby and me long enough for us to understand the situation." Sissy raised a hand to the neck of her ruffled blouse. "Abby and I were talking the other day about things here. What about one of your brothers or sisters taking a turn?"

"You know they have their own families." Annie heard a catch in her voice that revealed the truth behind her confidence.

"And you'll never have one at this rate," Sissy said. "You know, dear—"

The kettle's whistle halted her comment, and Annie spun around to pull it from the burner, praying she could control the emotion that rattled her.

As she made the tea, her thoughts dueled with the situation. Sissy was right. God meant the honoring part of His commandment for all children. Her four siblings had honored no one since their mother had died.

"Here you go," Annie said, trying to keep her voice light. She set the cup in front of Sissy and settled into the chair across from her.

Sissy took a careful sip of the hot tea, then placed the cup on the table. "I realize they all live away, but doesn't Susan live in Fremont? That's not so far that she couldn't come for a few days."

"We have a cousin in Fremont. Susan lives in White Cloud."

"That's not much farther." Sissy lowered her eyes and stared into her teacup.

Silence shrouded the room, and Annie wondered if the woman had fallen asleep or perhaps found something floating in her tea.

"Is something wrong, Sissy?"

Her head raised slowly. "Oh, no, dear. I was thinking about Ken and what a nice man he is. How you and he could spend time together...both being single. You know, for company." A melancholy look flooded her eyes.

Annie wondered about the two sisters who'd lived beside her family's home for so many years. "But you've never married, Sissy, and you and Abby do just fine."

Sissy gave a thoughtful nod before she spoke. "Yes. We're fine, but life can be more than fine, Annie." She fussed with the collar of her blouse again. "It can be wonderful, you know."

Holding her question poised in her thoughts, Annie

wondered if Sissy had some romantic tale to tell, but the older woman didn't continue, and Annie let it drop.

"Mrs. Bittle from church is coming next Thursday evening to sit with Pa while I go out for a birthday dinner." She hadn't wanted to share that news, but she felt as if she owed Sissy something.

The woman's face brightened. "A birthday dinner. With Ken?"

Annie nodded.

"Why, isn't that the nicest news." She reached across the table and patted Annie's hand. The translucent skin stretching across her fingers looked like crinkled tissue. "God has His way, Annie. Just remember that."

Annie smiled. She knew God had parted the Red Sea and spoken from a burning bush, but she wasn't sure God had a miracle for her.

Realizing she'd been gaping like a yokel, Annie closed her mouth. She'd seen the Grand Rapids Hotel from the outside, but had never imagined she'd be inside or eat in the elegant 1913 Room. Despite making her lack of social experience obvious, she let her gaze travel the surroundings—the elaborate flower-encircled fountain, the chandeliers, the heavy dark-hued draperies and crystal sconces adorning the walls.

Pleased Ken had chosen the restaurant, she rested her hand on the white linen and ran her finger along the edge of the black-and-white china. Her dating years had ended in her mid-twenties. Even then her social life had been simple—a movie, dinner at a local café. After her mother's death, her activities had been tied to church. Having dinner with an eligible man seemed out of reach...until today.

"This is lovely," she said finally. "I never expected anything so elegant."

Ken's gaze swept the surroundings. "It's got what you call atmosphere."

"Atmosphere," Annie said, and wondered what the atmosphere would cost Ken. As she had perused the menu, her gaze had swept over the prices. More than thirty dollars for filet of beef and Dover sole. In the end, when the waiter took the order, she let Ken make her choice. He knew what he could afford.

In the quiet, Annie gazed into his eyes and felt a tinge of elation skitter up her spine. It wasn't the birthday dinner so much as the company. For the first time in years, she felt like a woman. A woman escorted to dinner by a man. Something so normal, but so alien to her.

"What are you thinking?" he asked, his eyes glinting in the candlelight—eyes that looked sad so often.

"Thinking how nice this is. I feel like a grown-up."

"You *are* a grown-up. You're a woman who should have so much. A family of your own. One or two little ones maybe."

She gaped at him, then chuckled, wondering where that thought had come from. "A woman my age with little ones? I don't think so."

"Why not?"

''For one thing, I'd need a husband.''

He nodded, his eyes hooded. ''I suppose.''

Annie focused on her water goblet, wondering how the conversation had drifted to parenthood and marriage. Ken confused her. He was usually quiet and so much a loner, she wondered if she knew him at all.

Still a myriad of words slipped into Annie's thoughts. *Kind. Generous. Practical. Deep. Compassionate.* Yet beneath those qualities, she sensed something else. Something hidden and secret. He seemed nervous whenever she'd asked about his past. Evasive even. Why? What had happened that he wanted to avoid? To forget?

She resisted the thoughts that billowed through her mind and turned the conversation to other things. Finally the meals arrived, and she savored the grilled chicken in a sun-dried tomato pesto sauce that Ken had selected.

''Everything's excellent,'' she said, placing her knife and fork on the edge of her plate, then lifting her stemmed glass to sip the lemony ice water.

Ken looked at her pleasure-filled face, and his stomach tightened. ''I'm glad you're enjoying the meal.''

''I'm enjoying more than the meal, Ken. Thanks for giving me this nice gift.''

Her frank comment touched him, and he wanted to tell her that being with her was a gift. ''You're welcome,'' he said, controlling his emotions. She looked so lovely, and he recalled how he'd been startled by her appearance when she'd opened the front door when he'd arrived to pick her up. "Did I wish you a happy birthday?"

"I don't recall, but this evening makes it the happiest I can remember." Her gray eyes sparkled like moonlight on snow.

His chest tensed, recalling the moment she'd opened the door. The lamplight had glowed on the simple rose-colored dress nestling around her shapely body. He'd never seen her look so attractive.

Studying Annie now in the restaurant's dim lighting, Ken admired her flushed cheeks and her silhouetted features. A new awareness nudged his senses. The woman was beautiful inside and out.

"Did I tell you Sissy Hartmann brought over the soup as she'd promised?" Annie asked.

Grateful she'd changed the subject, Ken nodded. "You mentioned it on the telephone." He lifted his coffee cup and took a drink.

"I guess I did." An uneasy look slid across her face as if her brain had stopped creating conversation. His mind was as blank as hers.

Silence hung heavy over them, and Ken wondered if he'd made Annie uncomfortable or if she were only thinking.

"You know so much about me," Annie said finally. "You've never told me about yourself."

Startled by her persistence, Ken shifted his hands below the table afraid he'd give away his edginess. "Me?" He managed a chuckle. "Not much to tell."

"Sure there is. I don't know anything about you…except you're one of the nicest people I know."

Unaccustomed to compliments, Ken faltered with a response while his past ripped through him like buckshot. His body winced with a million stings and one large hole in his heart. "Thanks, but I'm not that nice."

A tiny grin curved her lips. "Don't push away compliments, Ken. You're terribly generous. Look at what you're doing tonight…just to wish me a happy birthday. You could spoil me."

He wished he could spoil her. Someone should. Admiring her in the dusky light, he longed to take her in his arms, but that happened only in dreams. Never in his lifetime.

Silence covered them for a moment, and he hoped he'd distracted her from pursuing the inevitable. One day he would have to tell her something about himself. Never the truth, but something.

"So…tell me," she insisted.

His hope slid to the floor.

"Really. There's not much to tell. I grew up in Cadillac, Michigan. Took a few classes after high school, then spent my life roaming from place to place. I never seem to settle down for long."

"How long have you lived in Loving?"

His chest ached with her innocent questions. "About five years."

"Just that long?" She looked at him as if amused. "I've lived here all my life. My parent always lived in Loving, too, and in the same house we're living in now."

Ken nodded, recounting in his mind how many

places he'd lived. What would it be like to live in one place for ten years? Fifteen? Forever?

He was lost in thought, and Annie's voice jarred him.

"Where did you live before Loving?" she asked.

He swallowed the bile that rose to his throat.

# Chapter Three

"I lived in Fremont," Ken said, managing to keep his voice calm.

"Fremont? Really? I have a cousin who lives there. Maybe you know her. Carol Danski."

His pulse escalated. "No, but it's a big town." But not big enough, he feared.

Annie shrugged. "I never see her…and Fremont's really close. But then, I rarely see…. Oh well, that's how families are. They drift."

"Who needs 'em?" Ken asked, pushing a light-hearted tone to his voice. If a loving God really dwelt in heaven, Ken wanted to send Him a prayer of thanks that Annie's family was distant. What would he do if she spoke with her cousin on a regular basis? His name might come into the conversation, and she'd remember him. He smothered his own skepticism. Fremont was a big town. Gossip didn't travel that far.

Annie gave him a warm smile. "Were you ever married?"

Her question startled him. "Married. No."

"Engaged?"

"Once."

"What happened?"

He wanted to stop her continual questions, but he didn't know how other than not answering. "Cheryl and I realized we'd made a mistake. You know how it is."

"Not really," she said, a faint grin catching her mouth. "I've never been involved. Dated, yes, but never anything serious."

He wished he'd lied. A lie would have been easier.

"Do you enjoy living here?" Her gaze searched his. "You're not planning to leave us, are you?"

Wanting to stop her questions, Ken slid his hand across the table and rested it on hers. "No plans to do that. At least not now."

Her gaze drifted to his hand, but she didn't pull away.

Worrying he'd make her uneasy, Ken moved his arm back, then raised his suit-jacket sleeve and eyed his watch. "You don't turn into a pumpkin, do you?"

Concern lashed her face "It's not midnight."

Her reaction made him chuckle. "No, it's only ten."

Annie studied him a moment causing his skin to prickle at the questioning look on her face.

"That laugh sounded nice. Why don't you smile more, Ken?" she asked. "It looks good on you."

Her question caught him off-guard. "Not a lot to smile about most of the time."

She didn't respond to that. Instead, she lowered her gaze and checked her own watch. "It is ten. The time flew."

"I figured you don't want to keep Mrs. Bittle out too late."

She sighed. "Thanks for remembering. I've had such a good time I forgot about her. I suppose we should go."

In a matter of moments, Ken had paid the bill and guided Annie to the exit.

The return ride to Loving was quiet. Ken hoped Annie was reliving the evening while he struggled with his thoughts. The conversation had left him uneasy and aware he couldn't hide his past forever. One day he needed to open up and tell Annie what happened. But not tonight. And if he faced the truth, probably never.

When Ken pulled into Annie's driveway, he opened the passenger door and walked her to the porch to say good night, but Annie paused.

"Would you like to come in?" she asked.

The invitation surprised him. "This late?"

She nodded. "Abby Hartmann made me a birthday cake. I thought maybe you'd like a piece."

The reference caused him to glance at the Victorian rooming house next door. "It's hard to turn down a piece of cake."

She grinned and motioned him through the door. Inside, after a few amiable words, Mrs. Bittle said good-night and left. Annie waited until she'd pulled away in her car, then turned and beckoned Ken to follow her.

In the kitchen, Annie motioned to a chair. "Relax."

When she turned back toward the counter, Ken leaned his shoulder against the door frame and eyed the two-layer cake iced with white frosting. While he waited, Annie took a knife from a drawer, then pulled two plates from a cabinet and sliced into the dessert. She lowered a piece to each plate, and when she finished, she ran her fingertip along the knife blade and slid the icing into her mouth.

Ken's chest tightened, startled by the deep longing to taste the sweetness on her lips. He forced his gaze away and slipped into the chair, reining in the feelings surging through him. She deserved so much, and he had nothing to offer her. Nothing.

"I can make coffee if you'd like," she said, turning to face him.

"I've had too much already. I won't sleep tonight." He knew he had other reasons for not sleeping as the feelings crashed around him.

"How about some milk?"

"Thanks. That sounds good."

She filled the glass, then handed it to him. "Let's sit in the living room. We might as well be comfortable."

He picked up the cake plate and followed her from the kitchen.

While they ate in silence, Ken eyed the room. He'd

never sat there before—only passed through. He guessed the decor had remained the same for years. The large overstuffed sofa and chair weighted the room with its dark fabric, and heavy draperies blocked the sunlight. So different from Annie.

Yet, as he scanned the walls, three small paintings caught his attention—their lightness and cheer not fitting in with the other room accessories. He set down his glass, rose, and crossed the room.

The largest painting was a garden bench surrounded by red and yellow flowers with a butterfly hovering above a blossom. Life and color soared from the artwork. He shifted to a watercolor—a pale yellow vase filled with bright tulips.

Before he focused on the third, he hesitated. Leaning closer to the painting, he saw the artist's marking. So simple: *Annie,* written in a delicate flourish.

He spun around. "Annie?" He pointed to her.

A soft flush rose up her neck in the lamplight, and she nodded.

"Annie, they're beautiful. I had no idea you were an artist."

She shook her head. "I wouldn't call me an artist."

"I would," he said.

She gave a one-shoulder shrug. "Thank you." Her voice was soft.

"You're welcome," he said, pivoting to view the walls around the room. "Have you painted others?"

She gestured toward the ceiling. "A whole attic full."

"Seriously?" His pulse tripped, witnessing a side of her he'd never considered.

"Seriously. Sailboats. Sunsets. More flowers."

He couldn't imagine works like these gathering dust in a loft. The talent could give her an outlet and contact with people. "You should sell them."

"You mean I should rent space at a gas station like the people who sell those black-velvet paintings?" She eyed him with an uneasy grin.

"Not quite." He returned to his seat, but paused before he sat. "Look. I'm practical. Don't forget this is a tourist town. People spend money like water when they're on vacation, and paintings like these could sell. Once you have a reputation, who knows what they would bring in?"

Purpose charged through him. Not money, but something more. A goal for Annie.

"I don't think so." She rose, ambled to the three paintings, then crossed her arms. "Look at them. They're flawed."

"Life's flawed. That's what makes them real." Ken's words punched his heart.

She studied the paintings while he rose and moved behind her, drinking in the scent of her fragrance and longing to pull the clasp from her hair and run his fingers through the golden strands. He hadn't touched a woman since Cheryl had walked out on him years ago. He'd had no desire to, until now. Forty-five and celibate.

But the past week had opened new emotions like a spade digging up uncultivated soil. A seed had been

planted that was pushing
ginning to uncurl in the sun.

His body twitched with aware
his misplaced thoughts back into
mind and motioned to the pictures.
Good lines and color. What's interesting
gestion of shape rather than reality. Not ab
truth. Not impressionistic. Just you. Annie.''

She turned and faced him, standing so clos
could kiss her without taking a step. Her ey
searched his while a warning signal screamed in his
head. He rested his hand on her shoulder to keep his
distance.

He felt her tremble beneath his palm, and her skin
colored in a delicate flush. Tonight he wanted to forget his own worries. Annie needed to be tuned in to
reality. She needed to realize she had something to
offer the world—something that could give her a little
personal happiness.

Ken wavered. Who was he anyway? An art connoisseur? A Romeo? Controlling his emotions, Ken
let his palm slip from her shoulder.

Annie's gaze followed his hand downward, then
she drew her focus back to his face, a look of disappointment in her eyes. ''I'm too old to follow silly
dreams, but thanks for the compliment.''

''That's the second time tonight you've said you're
too old for something.''

''I'm forty-three today. It's too late to start over. I
don't have time.''

''You have time,'' he said. ''You don't give your-

nd time. Wait

and he didn't
dy.

e a moment
lisappointed
how Annie's
surprise her.
Somerville and
op. He'd thought
terested in a local
catered to monied tourists. But the man said he wasn't interested in handling paintings and suggested Ken check out the Gift Gallery.

But that had proven as hopeless. "We aren't interested in consignment items," the store manager had said, "and with an unknown artist, we can't take a chance on buying her work."

Ken drew in a lengthy breath. He'd been so certain.

Unwilling to face another rejection, Ken turned the key in the ignition and headed for his next job. Standing beside the large sprayer that covered the trees with insecticides, he reviewed other shops in town that would be receptive to a local unknown artist.

Pulling back the hoses, he stopped a moment, wondering why he'd gotten involved in Annie's business in the first place. For one thing, he realized the woman had trickled into his system just like the chemicals he had been spraying. But another reason seemed less benevolent. If he worried about Annie's life, he didn't have to deal with his own. The realization sent his spirit on a downward spin.

Ken packed the hoses and his equipment, then headed for Washington Avenue to Annie's—his last job of the day. As he turned the corner, the sign for Loving Treasures caught his attention. Annie had worked at the shop before her father's illness. They had talked about it one day.

He slowed, realizing he'd be pushing his luck to the max. The boutique sold women's accessories—purses, scarves, shawls and jewelry. Women's things. Nothing at all like artwork. Still the owner knew Annie and was as generous as a baker's dozen.

Ken pulled into the parking lot. Outside, he eyed the display window. A dumb idea, but here he was. He took a deep breath as he looked down at his khaki pants and grass-stained shoes, wondering if he should wait or go inside while the spirit moved him.

He stomped his shoes against the concrete walk until particles of earth and grass fell off in misshapen clumps, then he pushed open the door.

The bell tinkled, and he stepped inside breathing in the scent of leather and a tinge of spicy perfume.

"May I help you?"

Ken turned toward the employees-only doorway and spotted Claire Dupre. She floated into the room in a billowing dark-green caftan splotched with colorful parrots. He could almost hear jungle drums. Pushing his grin back, he offered his hand. "Hi, Claire. I'm Ken Dewitt. We've met before."

She nodded. "Dewitt Landscaping. I've seen you at the Chamber of Commerce doings."

"Yes. On rare occasions."

She bustled toward the counter, and Ken followed.

"So what can I do for you? A gift for someone special?" Claire's painted cheeks lifted with her grin.

"I have a question," Ken said, wishing he'd thought things through more thoroughly.

"A question?" Her eyes sparked with good humor. "I suppose I can handle that, too."

"You know Annie O'Keefe? She worked for you a while ago."

"Annie. Yes indeed." Interest rose on Claire's face. "I hated to see her go, but she had to care for her father. I hear he's not doing well."

"He's not," Ken said, wondering where to go from there. He decided to press forward. "Did you know that Annie's an artist?"

"Artist?" Claire's head drew back in surprise. "No. Never heard that one."

"She paints watercolors of flowers and the lake." He gestured toward Lake Michigan only a short distance away. "Sailboats and sunsets. Nice pictures, and I suggested she try to sell some of them."

Claire's gaze shifted to her shelves and tables of leather goods, scarves and silk blouses as if wondering why he was telling her. With a look of great curiosity, she refocused on Ken. "Sell them? Yes. If they're good, she should do that."

"They're exceptional," he said, feeling defensive for no reason in particular. "What do you think?"

A puzzled frown edged her face. "Is that your question?"

"Well no," Ken said, wishing he'd rehearsed his dialogue. "I realize this is an accessory shop, but you have a great display window right here on Washington and you know Annie personally."

He rubbed the back of his neck, trying to relieve the tension. He was a man of few words, and today he felt horribly inept. "I thought maybe you'd show a couple of her pieces in your window. On consignment."

"Here?" Claire took another slow survey of her boutique. She tossed her flyaway hair behind her shoulders and lifted two long fingers to her lips as if in thought.

Ken's compulsive behavior rattled his usual quiet demeanor. He felt driven. "It's self-expression." Looking at Claire's eccentric get-up he thought she'd understand the meaning of self-expression.

"Hmm. I wonder." Her fire-engine-red nails tapped against her chin. "I don't know about this, Ken," she said finally. "I'd want to see some of the paintings." She nodded her head. "Tell her to stop by and show me what she has."

Ken nodded, figuring the conversation had gone better than he'd begun to expect. The shop had a perfect location—not too far from the water that attracted crowds and in the center of the tourist area. "I'll let her know."

Extending his hand, he clasped Claire's with a firm shake. "Thank you."

Ken hurried from the shop before Claire changed her mind. Once in the truck, he punched the door frame. He'd turned into Mary Poppins—without an umbrella. Why in the world had he allowed himself to get caught up in Annie's life?

He rubbed his fist, still feeling the sting, and questioned how pleased Annie would really be anyway. The dream had been his, not hers.

Hoping he hadn't overstepped their friendship, he headed down Washington to Annie's. Since she wasn't on the porch, Ken decided to contain his news about the boutique. This time he'd think it through.

He unloaded the equipment and headed up the driveway to the backyard, his thoughts on Annie and how she'd take what he'd done. When he'd worked his way back around to the front, Annie's voice brought him to a halt.

She stood in the doorway, gripping the screen as if the door were giving her strength.

As Ken neared, her pale tear-stained face and fear-filled eyes alarmed him. Leaving the spreader beside the steps, he bounded onto the porch and grasped her shoulders. "What is it, Annie?"

She fell against his chest, her body trembling. Loving the feeling, Ken held her there until her shaking lessened. Then, he eased her back to look in her eyes.

Her cheek quivered as her mouth formed the words. "It's Pa."

# Chapter Four

"Is he—?"

Annie's voice caught in her throat. "I just called EMS. I...I'm not sure, b-but I'm afraid he's gone."

"I'm so sorry," Ken said, his hands still gripping her arms.

As the condolence left him, Annie heard a siren wail in the distance and draw closer. When the red vehicle stopped in front, Annie pulled herself erect while Ken stepped to the side.

Two men jumped from the vehicle, grabbing their equipment and hurrying to the porch.

Annie beckoned them up the stairs, then went ahead. The clomp of their footsteps thudded through her like a tolling bell. Death. The solitude, the loss washed over her like an encroaching enemy.

One paramedic moved past her through the doorway. He knelt beside her father and leaned closer as if listening for his breathing. He grasped his wrist. "We have a faint pulse," he said, flagging the driver.

Hearing his words, Annie's heart lurched as the driver hurried forward with an oxygen tank, and as the paramedic attached it while he spoke to his partner. "Get the litter."

The driver darted from the room. His footsteps faded into the distance while Annie waited in panic until the man returned carrying a stretcher.

The two men slid the stretcher beneath her father, then connected the top and bottom, and after strapping him on, they lifted him with minute precision and eased through the doorway toward the stairs.

Annie followed them from the room, and Ken clasped her arm in the hallway. "I'll drive you...if you'd like."

"Thanks." Though Ken had done enough, she needed someone and his strength gave her comfort.

Ken hurried down the stairs behind her, and at the bottom, Annie grabbed her handbag, its weight heavy in her shaking hands, and headed to the ambulance.

Outside, sounds and colors melded to gray. The buzz of hovering neighbors, who gathered like greedy flies, faded beneath the pounding in her temples.

The Hartmann sisters reached her side, each wringing their hands and asking questions.

"He's alive," Annie answered, moving to get closer to the EMS van. Her heart raced, and aching and confused, Annie watched them settle her father inside the vehicle.

The driver jumped into the ambulance, and before

the paramedic closed the back doors, he called to Annie. "Follow us. North Ottawa County Hospital."

"On Sheldon Road," Annie said to Ken.

Ken grasped her arm and supported her into his truck. Her legs felt weighted as she lifted herself to the high seat. She clasped the seatbelt as Ken slammed the door and rounded the truck bed to climb into the driver's seat.

He backed around in the neighbor's driveway and followed the lights and siren out of Loving, heading along Lake Shore Avenue toward Grand Haven.

For the first time, Annie had a moment to face the truth. She'd spent much of her adult life caring for her father, and now…if his weakened pulse faded to nothing she'd feel lost—as if her own life had ended. What would she do?

Years ago, she'd had dreams, and, living in a small town, marriage and family had seemed her direction, following in her siblings' footsteps. Then she'd begun to paint—color, light, line-creating illusion. New worlds had opened to her, and she could spill her dreams and emotions into landscapes on canvas. No need to travel far away. Beauty lay at her fingertips.

But after her father had declined and her mother had died, Annie's world had grown smaller. She'd still painted, but her work was boxed and forgotten— like her dreams. She'd given up hope. Unbidden, she was struck with the thought, is this really what the Lord meant her to do? She'd felt compelled to honor her parents, but was this what honor meant? Maybe she'd used martyrdom to escape facing her own life…to avoid dealing with it. The possibility overwhelmed her.

Annie glanced at Ken sitting beside her in silence. Except for an occasional glance, he kept his eyes on the ambulance while Annie dropped her head against the headrest and drew in a ragged breath. She'd controlled her tears these last agonizing minutes, but she was losing the battle. Unharnessed, she let them flow down her cheeks and brushed them away with the back of her hand.

Ken's stomach twisted as he watched Annie's sorrow. He released the wheel with one hand and reached across the expanse of the bench seat to pat her arm, to offer her a comforting touch. He'd kept himself so distant from people—since Cheryl—he felt inadequate. Raw.

Annie glanced his way, her sad, gray eyes misted like a rainy sky.

Struggling to find something to say, Ken remained silent. He'd been riddled by mixed emotions since Annie had called to him from the porch—sorrow for her possible loss, yet gratitude for her release. With her father's death, Annie's struggle would be over. She would regain her freedom. Her life.

The words sounded brutal, but for the past year, Ken had watched Annie nail herself inside a few walls—her own coffin—to care for a man whose life had left little to admire…like Ken's own life.

The ambulance turned into the emergency entrance and Ken followed. As they pulled forward, a security guard flagged him on to the restricted parking area.

He waited long enough for Annie to exit, then followed the guard's directions and pulled into the lot.

In seconds, he found Annie inside talking with an intake nurse. Her father had already been whisked away through a set of double doors. Ken stood back, tangled in thoughts like tendrils—his past, present, future.

Like Annie, he'd found his own life taken away, boxed behind four walls—but one with bars—walls not totally of his making. Circumstances of a foolish teen surrounded by unforgiving adults. A father who said he'd gotten what he deserved and a mother who'd looked at him with frightened eyes.

He'd watched his friends walk away, their slates wiped clean, but not his. Like Annie, he suffered the consequences of others who should have borne the weight. Annie had siblings, people who'd allowed her to carry the full load as he'd carried the full load for his friends.

"Ken?"

He jumped, hearing his name.

Annie beckoned to him. "They told us to sit in the waiting room. It'll be a few minutes."

Ken brushed his fingers along his jaw, feeling a growth of whiskers. The prickle seemed the only real thing about the moment. He walked beside Annie until she settled into a seat near the doorway, her face gray as a prison wall.

Sinking in a seat beside her, Ken slid his palm over her hand as she gripped the arm rest. No words came. No words that reflected the truth of her sadness. Comments like *sorry* and *maybe* had no permission to break the hush.

Annie shifted to face him while his hand still rested on hers. "I don't know what to do. I'm at a loss right now."

"You don't have to think or talk. Let's wait and see what happens." The response seemed right to Ken. Words without false hope.

"I need to call the family. They should know Pa is in the hospital."

Ken nodded, wondering if they would come to visit even if she called. He'd heard Annie mention their names, but he'd never seen them. Never heard they'd come for a visit.

"Would you like me to call someone?" Ken asked, slipping his hand in his pocket to see if he had change.

She shook her head. "I'll wait to see what—"

"Family of Roy O'Keefe."

Annie jumped at the sound, and Ken lifted his hand from hers. "You go ahead. I'll wait here."

She rose, shaking her head. "No. Please come."

Slowed by reluctance, Ken eased upward and followed her to the doorway. He stood behind her as the doctor whispered the pronouncement. "I'm sorry. We did all we could, but it was too late."

As if prepared for the outcome, Annie drew up her shoulders and nodded her head.

*I'm sorry,* the doctor had said. Ken felt sorry, too, for Annie's grief. For her loss, but not for Annie.

No tears came until the physician had gone. Then Annie rested her head against his chest and wept.

"Everything will be okay," Ken whispered, watching the bars of her prison slide open and Annie step out into the fresh air.

Annie called her siblings. She closed her personal phone book and pushed the telephone farther back on the table. They'd heard her message with quiet voices and dry eyes. She'd heard no grief, no sense of loss...except from the second oldest, Bill. And his sorrow seemed more for her than for the loss of their father.

Other than her oldest brother, Roy, they had all promised to arrive the day after tomorrow, but the visitation and funeral plans had to be done in the morning. She listened to the silence, a quiet she would learn to know, but for now she hated it.

As a Christian she should rejoice that her father had gone to heaven. Instead, she felt no victory for herself in his passing, only a purposeless life. She'd allowed the world to pass her by. While her father found a home in heaven, Annie faced the unknown on earth.

Shame crept into her heart. She needed to re-find her life. Ken had already intimated that. She knew it was true, but today she let self-pity cover her.

Resting her chin on her hand, Annie thought a moment, then pulled the telephone closer. Ken had told her to call if she needed him. She needed someone. The ludicrous situation roused her. She had acquaintances at church…and neighbors, too. Sissy and Abby Hartmann and others, but she needed her landscaper for company? For support?

Except that wasn't the truth. Ken had become more to her than that. Much more. He'd held her in his arms when she had fallen apart seeing her father's dying breaths. He'd patted her arm on the way to the hospital and covered her hand with his in the waiting room. Ken had become her friend. Her closest friend.

And now she needed him.

Annie looked at his business card and punched in his cell phone number. If he were working, he'd return her call. She left a voice mail message, then hung up and waited.

When the telephone rang, Annie felt whole.

"Saying thank you seems so feeble for all you've done," Annie said, unlocking the door and pushing it open, grateful that he'd spent the difficult day with her.

"It's nothing," he said, holding the screen door.

"Come in." She stood back to let him inside.

Ken glanced at his wristwatch, then nodded.

Annie motioned toward the living room. "Have a seat and let me run upstairs a minute. I'll be right back."

Before she took a step, the doorbell rang. Surprised, Annie opened it and faced two women holding bowls.

"You can use these, I'm sure," one woman said, handing her the casserole. Annie gazed at the other woman extending a second dish. Before she had time to think, Ken stepped forward.

"Let me help," he said, grasping the last container.

Annie thanked the women and closed the door. "What will I do with all this?" she asked heading for the kitchen, thinking she might never eat again.

Ken followed her and waited while she opened the refrigerator. She slid in the casserole, then turned to take the second.

Ken observed her with a shrouded gaze. His face had given her no clue to his feelings. He'd spent the afternoon with her and the funeral director as she signed papers and provided the obituary information. Annie had been grateful her father had a grave plot beside her mother. It meant she had one less thing to worry about.

Ken had helped her select her father's clothing—a gray suit she hadn't seen him wear in years. A shirt and tie. She'd even thrown shoes in the bag. Shoes? She hadn't reasoned why she'd brought them along. Her father had no need for them now. Ken had carried the garments into the funeral home for her. He'd even helped her select the memory and acknowledgment cards.

Observing his quietness, Annie's stomach twisted and the emotion she'd pushed back inside rose to the surface. Tears welled in her eyes, and she covered them with her hand and returned her gaze to the contents of the refrigerator.

But before she could get anything in focus, the door nudged from her hand and closed, and Ken turned her to face him. He lifted a roughened finger and brushed the tears from her eyes, then leaned down to kiss her cheek. The gesture came as an unexpected surprise, both welcome and confusing.

Annie gazed into his eyes, seeing depths as dark and profound as the water of Lake Michigan. She raised her hand and cupped his cheek against her fingers, felt the deep cleft in his chin. The stubble of whiskers felt raspy beneath her palm, but the feel gave her strength as if this silent-as-stone man was her shield. Her protection.

She had no words to respond to his simple kiss. She had questions. Did he feel pity for her? Did her sorrow touch his heart from a past loss of his own? Did he kiss her as a friend or…?

Before she could silence her thoughts, the doorbell rang a second time. "More food, I'm afraid."

"I'll get it," Ken said, vanishing through the doorway before she could stop him.

Annie listened with half an ear until Abby and Sissy's voices drew nearer following Ken back into the kitchen.

"Now don't worry, dear," Sissy said, setting a pie on the counter, "we've planned a luncheon after the funeral."

Clearer understanding settled in Annie's mind. She realized the reason for the dishes the neighbors had brought over.

"The neighbors have all volunteered," Abby said. "We'll bring over our tea set. It's sterling silver."

Their words struck her. She had given no thought

to a luncheon following the service. "That's kind of you."

"Shush," Sissy said. "It's the least we can do. We'll take care of everything."

Abby nodded, still holding a pie tin. "While we're at the service, a couple of church ladies will come in to set out the luncheon."

She extended the dessert, and Annie took it from her, sliding it beside the others.

"I don't know what I'd do without good neighbors," Annie said, giving each sister a hug.

"Oh, you'd manage, but we want to make things a little easier," Sissy said.

Abby's gaze had redirected itself. "And you have this nice man here to help you, too."

Annie ignored the comment. Any response would only ascertain that the sisters' news would travel more quickly.

To herd them toward the doorway, Annie stepped forward. "As you can see, we just got home, and I have so much to do."

"Don't let us stop you then, dear," Abby said. "Come along, Sister." She steered Sissy through the doorway, then lingered a moment taking in all that she saw. "Our thoughts and prayers are with you."

"Thanks," Annie said, moving in their direction.

Ken cut her off and walked the sisters to the front door in her place. In a moment, he returned, a grin curving his mouth. A grin that gave Annie hope for a better day.

"What?" she asked.

"Nothing. I just have to laugh."

"I'm glad. We've had very little to smile about today."

Annie pulled out the coffee pot and filled the basket with grounds. The homey fragrance rose, giving her a sense of reality. Pushing the sadness aside, Annie gestured toward the living room. "Why not have a seat and I'll make another attempt at taking off my shoes. Then we can talk."

Ken eyed her black pumps, a faint grin spreading across his face before he vanished through the doorway.

His grin warmed her as his presence did so often. She'd realized throughout the past two days that the Lord had sent him to be her friend when she needed one most. What would she have done without his steady company and his quiet wisdom?

# *Chapter Five*

"**Y**our family will be here tomorrow?" Ken asked, his fingers enveloping a coffee mug.

"Except for my oldest brother, Roy. He's not coming." Disappointment flooded her face.

Ken opened his mouth to question why, but Annie's look stopped him.

"Don't ask," she said, rubbing the back of her neck.

"You look tired," Ken said, shifting from the chair to the sofa to sit beside her.

He'd watched the tension building in her posture, the lines deepening in her face. Without asking, he turned her so he could reach her shoulders with both hands. He plied his fingers along the cords of her neck and down her spine, working in circles above her shoulder blades where muscles lay bound as tight as seaman's knots.

He heard Annie's gratifying moans of relief as he

worked his thumbs along her back to the hollow of her spine. The sounds awakened his senses. She seemed to relax, and she let her head droop forward, swaying her neck in rhythm to his touch. He could imagine caressing her smooth, soft skin and kissing her slender neck.

"Feel better?" he asked, tightening the reins of his emotions, alarmed that his ministration had aroused a deep desire to hold her in his arms.

She rolled out an um-hum along with a deep sigh in response. "Thank you."

"You're more than welcome." Really, he wanted to thank her for reviving his humdrum life—for restoring his pleasure in waking each morning.

With a gentle touch, he drew her toward him. "I want you to get a good night's rest so you'll be ready for tomorrow."

Her eyelids drooped and she gave a faint nod.

He brushed her cheek with his fingertips. "I know it'll be difficult."

She looked at him, her eyes so trusting, and he realized he had to tell her what he'd decided. "I won't be here tomorrow. I think you need to deal with your family without my interference. I have little patience with uncaring loved ones. I lived that once. I don't want to see it again."

A frown settled on her forehead. "I know I'm strong. I've put up with a lot over the years, but it's nice to have a friend."

A friend. More than a friend. It sneaked up on him when he wasn't looking.

"Will you come in the morning to give me moral support before they get here?" she asked.

"You don't need me for moral support. Once they're here and you have a chance to talk, I think things will make more sense to everyone."

"You have more faith than I do, Ken." She averted his gaze. "I've been a Christian all my life, but lately, I've watched myself drift. I attend worship most of the time, but I can't seem to cling to God's promises. I believe in heaven and hell. I believe in salvation, but...I've prayed—prayed until I turned purple—and I've never felt God's answer."

"I can't help you there, Annie. I don't even pray. But I know that a person can want something so badly he can taste it, and it may never happen." The words stung as they left his mouth, his own life filled in the blanks that he left in his words.

"What a person wants may hurt someone else," he added. "That's because people can't see the whole picture."

Annie smiled. "You learned that in the Bible. It's from First Corinthians. 'Now we see but a poor reflection as in a mirror; then we shall see face to face. Now I know in part; then I shall know fully.'"

"Not the Bible, Annie. It's common sense."

"Did you ever go to church?"

"Yes." A rush of memory overwhelmed him. He pictured himself jammed between his father and mother. The black Bible in his father's thick fingers. A Bible his father had used to beat him. *Spare the rod and spoil the child.* He remembered his father's husky voice hissing the words in his face.

"Sunday school?" Annie asked.

"When I was young, with my mother." He wanted to tell her when he was old enough to rebel he refused to go.

"Those lessons stick with you, I think. I remember so much from my Sunday-school days."

Ken shook his head. "To me, it's that 'poor reflection' in the mirror, you mentioned. I have only faint recollections."

"In your mind, maybe. But God's Word settles in your soul."

Ken watched her expression grow serious. He realized the hope she denied still lived in her heart. "I'm not sure what's in my soul." He wasn't even sure he had one. A heart, yes. He felt anguish and sorrow. But the soul?

"The end of that verse is my favorite," Annie said, her expression content.

"You have a good memory."

She grinned. "Want to hear it?"

"Why not?"

"'And now these three remain: faith, hope and love. But the greatest of these is love.' That's how the verse ends."

Faith, hope and love? He wondered if he'd ever experience any of them fully.

"I didn't know you were a romantic, Annie."

"I'm not."

Ken saw the look in her eyes that denied what

she'd said, and he longed to know what she saw in his. Unable to control his reaction, he leaned over and kissed her cheek.

Footsteps on the front porch roused Annie from her chair. She hadn't heard the car pull up in front, but she knew from the sound that her sisters had arrived.

She'd hoped that Ken would have surprised her and shown up as she'd hinted, but she understood. He seemed to withdraw around people, especially ones he didn't know.

Annie opened the door and waited while her sisters pulled their overnight bags from the trunk. They'd obviously left children and husbands home.

As Donna climbed the steps, Annie pushed open the screen door. "How was the trip?"

Donna shook her head. "I had to listen to Susan's complaints all the way here. Other than that it was fine."

Susan followed close behind, her own head shaking. "Talk about whining." She gave her head a quick tilt toward Donna. "I'm no competition."

They both swept past Annie through the doorway and stopped in the foyer. No greeting. No moment of quiet remembrance. Only a let's-get-this-business-over-with attitude.

Annie closed the door to hold in the air-conditioning and gestured toward the staircase. "You can share your old bedroom. Or one of you can sleep in Pa's room, if you don't mind a hospital bed."

They both arched an eyebrow and headed up the

stairs while Annie watched from below. She needed a moment's reprieve to collect her thoughts.

In a few moments, their clomping footsteps echoed in the hallway, and Annie rose to meet them. "Are you hungry? The neighbors have sent over a ton of food."

"I could eat something," Susan said, swinging toward the kitchen doorway. Her navy slacks and co-ordinated top showed off the slender frame Annie had always envied. Susan even wore an appropriate single strand of pearls.

Donna, looking more harried, followed Susan through the doorway, but Annie stayed in the living room, waiting. Her stomach churned and the thought of food sickened her.

Dishes rattled and cabinets banged until silence won the battle. Then only an occasional female voice drifted in from the kitchen along with a cell phone conversation. Annie heard Susan's voice directing some kind of business with controlled authority.

Annie leaned her head against the sofa back and gazed at the paintings on the wall. If only she could climb inside and hide among the flowers or sail off into the sunset.

"Who made the pie?" Donna asked, coming through the doorway with a glass of iced tea.

"The Hartmann sisters. They brought two over yesterday."

Donna settled into a chair, staring at her drink and avoiding Annie's gaze.

Annie waited, unwilling to initiate any conversation until she sensed the direction in which things would go. Before long, Susan ambled into the room, carrying a small brandy-snifter—one that had been pushed far back in an upper cupboard.

"Sherry," Susan said, lifting the glass as in a toast. "I wonder how long it's been in the cabinet."

Annie arched a brow. "Isn't it a little early to start drinking?"

Susan rammed the glass onto a lamp table and sank into the chair beside it. "No. I don't think so."

Annie shrugged, wishing she'd kept her mouth shut as she meant to do.

Donna seemed to ignore the confrontation and stared at her fingernails. Finally she dropped her hand in her lap and said, "What's the plan?"

"Plan?" Annie asked, lost for a moment in her meaning.

"She means, when's the visitation? I hope you took care of everything," Susan said.

Annie pushed a stray hair from her face. Hadn't she always taken care of everything? "Visitation is today. Three to eight. Pa doesn't have many friends anymore, so, other than church people, I don't think we'll have a big crowd."

"That's a relief," Susan said. "We don't have to drag this thing out. The funeral's at the church?"

"At ten in the morning," Annie said.

"Good, then we can be on our way early," Susan said.

"The neighbors have planned a luncheon for us afterward. Here."

"A luncheon?" Susan's face pinched with disagreement.

Silence settled over them until Donna shifted and cleared her throat.

"I know this must be hard for you, Annie." Donna's expression registered the first note of empathy Annie had witnessed. "You spent your life rescuing dad when no one else would."

Susan snorted. "That's because the rest of us had better sense." She glowered in Annie's direction. "And don't start quoting the Bible."

Donna slapped her hand against the chair arm. "Susan, you don't have to be unkind, and you know the Bible makes sense. Annie did what she thought was right." She checked her nails again, and turned to Annie. "What will you do now?"

Amid the ping-pong of comments, Donna's inquiry sent Annie a curve. "Good question. I've been asking myself the same thing. I had to quit my job when Pa got really bad, so I suppose I'll have to find work."

"We don't want a pity party, Annie," Susan said. "You chose to stay here. As Mom always said, you made your bed and now you have to lie in it."

"Donna asked the question, Susan. I'm not complaining." Annie ran her hand along the back of her neck as if checking her hair clip, but she longed for Ken's strong hands to knead the tension from her shoulders. "I'll have to get things in order here, and then carve a new life for myself."

The thought of carving something cut through Annie's mind. Her sister's pearl-draped throat, for one.

The evil thought made her smile inside, but, as quickly, caused her to send up a prayer. *Patience, Lord.*

Donna took a sip of the tea and held the glass between her hands as if looking into a crystal ball. "When you think about it, Annie, you've had it pretty easy. No kids to worry about, no husband to please...or try to please." She rolled her eyes. "You didn't even have to work the past couple of years."

"I wouldn't call that easy," Annie said. "Pa was still as tough as nails to—"

"Speaking of nails," Donna said, "I haven't had mine done in weeks." She held her hand out for her sisters to take a look.

"I hope Pa's death didn't cut into your manicure appointment," Annie said, wanting to slam her hand over her mouth, but the words had already escaped.

"Look," Susan said. "Let's not get testy. We have too much to do before we leave for the funeral home. We need to find Pa's papers. Insurance, and I know he had a will."

"He kept things in a strong box in his room," Annie said. "The key's on his dresser, I think."

Donna leaned forward. "Susan, don't you think that could wait?"

"For what?" Susan asked. "We might as well know our share." She turned to Annie. "We'll need to get the house appraised."

The house? Annie's chest knotted until she couldn't breathe.

* * *

Ken stood in the visitation-room doorway, sizing up the situation. Annie stood by the casket. His chest tightened, seeing her there alone. He let his gaze sweep the room, recognizing a couple of towns-people, probably from the church, but when he viewed the two women sitting together on a side sofa, he paused. Annie's sisters. He saw the resemblance. Though in his opinion, Annie won the beauty contest hands down.

He crossed the carpet and stepped behind Annie. When he put his hand on her arm, she jumped.

"Ken." A look of relief flooded her face. "I didn't know if you'd come."

He gave her arm a squeeze. "I didn't say I wouldn't be here." He moved beside her and looked down on the thin, gnarled face of Roy O'Keefe. The hard younger years had taken a toll on him, and the later ones had begun to take their toll on Annie.

"I'm glad you came," Annie said, her hands clasped in front of her clutching a white handkerchief.

"How are things going?"

She shook her head almost imperceptibly. "Don't ask."

"That bad?"

She nodded.

Anger rose up his back like quicksand—black and smothering. He'd endured hurt and abandonment years earlier, and maybe he'd deserved it, some of it, but not Annie. She'd given her life to make her fa-ther's years tolerable.

He did a slow turn and eyed the two women, huddled together in private conversation. In his mind, they should have been standing with Annie, giving her support. Instead, they'd paired up against her. The scene felt too familiar, and Ken closed his eyes to control the old anger from taking over.

Now he wished he'd gone to Annie's that morning. What could he have done? Nothing, perhaps. The whole situation was none of his business. Yet, Christian or not, he wanted to do the right thing. To show a little human kindness.

"What can I do?" he asked, close to her ear.

"Probably nothing, but thanks." She kept her eyes straight ahead.

"Is your brother here?"

"Not yet. Later…I think."

"I'm coming to your house tonight. After the visitation."

"I'd like that, but I doubt if it will make any difference. They're worse than I remembered."

"I'll see for myself."

Annie grabbed his arm. "Let me introduce you."

Ken's back tightened as she guided him toward the two women. Whether it was caused by their treatment of Annie or worry that he might be recognized by one of them, he didn't know.

Ken had learned to live in fear—fear that his past would catch up with him and send him running again. He'd moved more than once to avoid the staring eyes and flapping tongues of small-town people who labeled him the ex-con.

The title stabbed through his mind. He'd been a

teen and had destroyed property. Yes, wrong, but he'd paid a price far beyond his deed. He'd been made an example in the town. A warning to children not to misbehave, and he'd gone to prison with no support from his father or defense from the friends who'd been with him and joined in the foray. The painful memory washed over him.

Dear Annie. She'd been ganged up on, too. The knowledge hurt his heart more deeply than his own sorrow.

Ken gathered his wits and allowed Annie to guide him to her sisters' sides. He forced a pleasant expression as the two women looked at him with curious eyes.

"Susan. Donna. This is my friend, Ken Dewitt."

He held his breath, waiting. Foolish. It had all happened so long ago, but the fear always slithered down his back without his control.

"A friend of Annie's. How nice to meet you," Susan said, rising and extending her hand.

Susan reeked of charm and business, like an oversolicitous salesclerk. Ken took her hand, then Donna's. She gave him a simple smile. "I'm glad to meet you."

Ken nodded as a faint musical jangle invaded the hush. Susan dropped to the chair and grabbed her purse. Feeling inside she pulled out a cell phone, then rose and walked away, speaking in a hushed tone.

Wanting to give Susan a swift kick, Ken stepped back while Annie spoke to a new arrival. When the time seemed right, Ken turned away and found a chair where he could observe and think. One brother had refused to come. Two sisters appeared to conspire together, and the other brother hadn't arrived yet. What did he hold in store?

Annie moved away to greet another visitor, and Ken's gaze drifted to the casket. A spray of red roses covered the bronze top with a ribbon saying *Dear Father*. Ken's chest tightened, knowing Annie had selected the words. Inside, against the cream lining, Ken's gaze fell upon a simple cross.

A cross. Annie's life had been a cross. She'd had to bear the weight alone. His mind drifted back to Sunday school. As Annie had said, he remembered the stories of Jesus's death. He'd heard them in Sunday school and in his father's nightly readings—readings that had lasted so long his eyelids would close and the thick, black Bible would slam against the table to awaken him.

Ken recalled a man who'd been coerced into carrying Jesus's cross. Simon came to mind. Ken had often wished he could have accomplished some kind of penitential deed as Simon had. Something to shed his past. To ease his abandonment. To pay for his sins. To heal his heart.

Hoping Annie's brother would arrive soon, Ken watched her sisters' interactions. Bill seemed to be Ken's only hope. *If you're listening, Lord,* Ken said to himself, *let Bill be a Simon for Annie. Let him carry her burden.*

As the thought flew heavenward, Ken reeled. Where had that come from? A prayer? He hadn't prayed in years.

# Chapter Six

Standing in the kitchen rinsing dishes, Annie listened to the living-room conversation that pierced the silence. After they'd returned from the funeral home visitation, Susan had found the key and the strong box. Her sisters had gathered round, plowing through their father's papers.

Silent, Ken stood beside her and fed the rinsed plates and silverware into the dishwasher. He'd said little as she rode back to the house with him from the funeral home. Longing to know his thoughts, she tried to penetrate his solitude, but his comments were noncommittal, as if he had no right to an opinion.

"Just about finished," Annie said, motioning toward the living room. "Go ahead. I'll be there in a minute."

Ken shrugged and went ahead of her through the doorway.

When Ken reached the living room, Annie heard

the overly polite comments from her sisters while she stood inside the kitchen doorway, trying to get her bearings. One thing they had was social skills. She bowed her head and closed her eyes. Since her father's death, Annie had faced a Christian reality. When times get tough, people turn to the Lord. How often she'd forgotten to pray, forgotten to give thanks, forgotten to let God lift her burdens.

But not today. She asked for forgiveness first—forgiveness for pushing the Lord aside. Then she prayed for God's will. Whatever happened she asked for strength to bear up under it. She'd been strong for years until the past months, when the pressure seemed to undo her. Perhaps it was longer than that—her fortieth birthday. A time when she realized child-bearing would be nearly impossible. When she realized she'd spend her life alone. No one's wife. No one's mother. Her dream of holding her own baby in her arms faded. She had so little time left and so little hope.

Ken's face entered her mind, his eyes filled with dark thoughts—thoughts that scared her sometimes. But beneath his veiled reflections, Annie cared about him. Too much. He'd been kind, tender in his concern, but she sensed he had no plans to move their relationship beyond friendship. She closed her eyes, letting his image fade like worn fabric. Then opening them again, Annie drew in a deep breath and strode into the living room, hoping her pretense of confidence looked real.

"Anyone want dessert?" she asked, facing her sisters who sat like vultures on each side of the strong box, papers strewn over the center cushion.

"No thanks," Susan said, directing her bright smile toward Ken. "I have to watch my girlish figure."

Donna rolled her eyes. "Maybe later. Thanks."

"Dad has a small insurance policy," Susan said, staring at a creased document. "I'm guessing it's worth about four thousand. That's barely enough to cover funeral expenses."

"Not even barely," Annie said.

Both sisters lifted their eyes, their expressions shifting to a frown.

"How much did you spend, Annie?" Donna asked.

"I didn't spend anything. That's how much funerals cost." She glanced at Ken, wishing he'd tell them she'd selected nearly the bottom of the line on everything.

Ken sat, resting his elbows on his knees, his eyes focused on the floor.

"We found the will," Susan said, waving the papers in her hand. "Equal split. Five ways."

Annie's heart sank. She had never talked with her father about a will. Never given it much thought... until now.

"I suppose tomorrow we should call someone for an appraisal," Donna said. "Do you know anyone in real estate?" Her gaze drifted from Annie to Ken.

Ken didn't move.

Annie shook her head.

"Good idea," Susan said. "We need to get things rolling."

"Why are you in such a hurry?" Ken asked.

His voice startled Annie, and she turned to look at him. His face looked flushed and the dark emotion in his eyes sparked with fire.

"No hurry," Susan said, giving him a look that meant this was none of his business.

Ken rose. "I think I'll have a piece of that pie." He fled the room like a man pursued.

Susan and Donna returned their attention to the strong box, and Annie took advantage of their distraction to follow Ken.

When she came through the doorway, he faced the counter, his hands gripping the edge, his head lowered.

"Ken?"

He didn't turn around, but only shook his head.

"I'm sorry. They're rude."

He swung around to face her, his fists clenched. "You can't just sit there and let them take everything without a fight, Annie. They're selfish and unthinking."

"What do you expect me to do?"

He closed the distance between them and grasped her shoulders. "Speak your mind. Tell them you've devoted your life to your father while they didn't bear one ounce of the burden. Tell them this house is yours. It's payment for the years you gave to your father that they didn't have to."

Annie reeled back, startled by the barrage of words. In all the time she'd known him, Ken had never displayed such intense emotion. "I chose to be here."

"You chose by default. Tell them you'll take them to court and contest the will."

"Court? I can't do that. They're my family."

"One-sided."

Tears rose in her eyes. Though he'd spoken the truth, the truth hurt. "Ken, I appreciate your concern, but I'm letting God be in charge. If my father wanted me to have the house, he'd have put it in the will."

"I let God be in charge once and I lost. I was too dumb and stupid to know I had to fight for the truth."

"I'm sorry about your problem...but this is how I have to handle it. I appreciate your friendship. I appreciate your trying to help, but you don't understand. This is really none of your business."

Ken looked as if he'd been slapped. He turned, and without saying goodbye, he headed for the back entry and stepped out the door.

The door didn't slam, but Annie's heart whacked against her chest louder than a sonic boom. She'd never felt so alone.

Ken stood in Annie's backyard, drawing in the fresh air and easing the sting of her words. She was right. It was none of his business, but he wouldn't be a man if he stood by and watched her being mistreated without saying something.

He stepped out of the shadow and headed around the house toward his car while his mind drifted back. Had he been older years ago, he would have found a lawyer who understood. He hadn't been alone in his actions then. Three goading friends had been at his

side, smashing furniture, swilling liquor, shouting ob-
scenities. He'd been drunk. Not the first time. But
drunker, perhaps, than he'd ever been.

Eighteen meant freedom. Freedom from his father's
tyranny. Poor excuse, but the truth. He'd learned, and
today he never touched a drop. But today was too
late.

In his mind, Annie stood alone as he had. Not her
father saying she was only getting what she deserved,
but sisters insinuating the same idea. Maybe a
brother…if he ever arrived. She had carried the
weight, and now she would buckle under the pressure
and be crushed by their selfishness. He was glad he'd
left. Watching the hurt only perpetuated his own sorrow.

When he reached the car, Ken slid inside, wondering what to do. Where to go. Home seemed the only
answer. He turned the key in the ignition and pulled
away, his eager eyes watching the windows as he
turned around in the driveway, wondering if Annie
were watching with second thoughts.

"Annie's not a weak woman," he said to no one,
"but she needs help." On the street, he hit the turn
signal to make a left and pulled up to the light. The
steady tick matched the beat of his heart. *Lord, Annie
thinks a kindly God is up there. Maybe You are. I
can't do what needs to be done so it's up to You.*

The light changed and he turned the corner, his
mind tumbling with alien thoughts and feelings.
Somewhere in his head he sent up an amen. Prayers
ended with an amen. He knew that.

At home, Ken drank a glass of milk, then lay in bed tossing and turning until the black sky brightened to gray. Finally sleep overtook him.

An incessant ringing jarred him awake, and he sat up, rubbing his face and staring with blurry eyes at the alarm clock. He hit the button, but the pealing continued. The phone. He rolled over to reach the night stand and grasped the receiver, whispering a throaty hello.

"Ken?"

Annie's soft voice wove through the line to his ear.

"Annie." He propped himself on one elbow.

"I'm sorry. I was wrong last night."

"It's okay."

"No. It's not okay. It was uncalled for. I asked you for help, and you were only doing what a friend would do."

He didn't know how to respond. Whether to let it pass and agree or to try to explain. A deep need to tell her his past flooded over him. To tell her why her family's treatment of her stabbed him so deeply...but he remembered trusting Cheryl. He remembered swallowing his fear and grasping courage to be honest with her. He remembered Cheryl turning her back and walking away. She wanted nothing to do with an ex-con. No criminal would be the father to her children.

"Ken?"

"I'm here."

"Will you come today? To the funeral? I could use a shoulder to cry on."

His heart tripped against his chest, but the answer

came without question. "I'll be there, Annie. And I promise to keep my mouth shut. This is your business, not mine. I—"

"Please don't—"

"No. You're right about that. It's none of my business. Put your trust wherever you want. In the Lord if that's right for you." He could imagine her expression as she weighed what he'd said. "I'll be there."

"Thank you," she said, a deep sadness filling her voice.

The telephone disconnected, and Ken sat for a moment on the edge of the bed, holding the receiver. He leaned over and placed it back on the cradle.

Reality washed over him. He wasn't talking about a friendship anymore. Annie had become far more to him than a friend. Even the crinkles around her eyes made her dearer. She'd become a woman he cared about more than he wanted. Her gentle face, those eyes that looked into his soul...a soul he wondered about.

*Put your trust...in the Lord if that's right for you,* he'd said to her, but hadn't he done the same recently. Hadn't he sent up a prayer asking God to help Annie? Where had all of that come from? Faith? He hadn't had faith since he was a kid. But Annie did...and he respected her. He admired her. He recalled Annie saying God's Word settles in your soul.

Could it be?

Annie looked out the window, watching cars line the street as church members and friends came through the door following the funeral. Neighbors made their way on foot, adding more dishes to the already wide array of casseroles, salads and meat platters.

Abby and Sissy had come early with their silver tea set and arranged it on the dining-room buffet along with desserts and small paper plates.

The refrigerator door swung open and closed, items being added as people brought them and removed as things were remembered—the pickle dish, the butter and creamer.

Annie caught Ken's attention and flagged him to her. "Could you help me bring up some folding chairs from the basement?"

"Let me get your brother to help."

"I'll show you now and he can help if we need more." She motioned him to follow her down the steps, veiling the need to see him alone. They'd had no time together in private, and she needed only a minute to apologize again and thank him for his caring ways.

On the stairs, she snapped on the light, and at the bottom, sunshine from outside seeped through the small windows. Annie crossed the gray concrete to a niche under the stairs. "They're here, but—" She stopped as Ken stepped beside her. "I really asked you to come down because I want to talk with you alone."

"Did I do something wrong again?"

"No. You did something right." She turned to face

him, longing to wrap her arms around his strong frame. "You did nothing wrong before, Ken. It's me." She struggled with the words. "I couldn't get through this without you. I've been on my own for so long, and I can't tell you how good it feels to have a friend. I know you're right. I should fight for this house…but—"

Before she finished the sentence, Ken stopped her. "Annie, please, that's your decision. I'm talking through my own horrible experience. We don't have time down here to talk, but I hope you can forgive me for my attitude. My father was a fire-and-brimstone believer. He was volatile and thought religion gave him permission to dominate and punish. My mother was a quiet women—a believer, but she was as intimidated as I was."

Annie placed a finger across his lips. "You don't have to—"

"If you see where I'm coming from, you'll understand why I'm a little warped about your family and their attitude. It's too close to home for me."

He placed his arms on her shoulders and drew her closer. "Annie, all you have to know is you're a special lady. I told you this morning you don't have to thank me. I want to be here."

She reached up and brushed her fingers along his temple, noticing a few gray hairs hiding among the dark brown. She glided her hand downward and cradled his cheek in her palm. "Oh, Ken, what can I say to…"

Annie's voice faded away as she tried to control

the tears that pushed behind her eyes. She gave an understanding nod and eased away. The tears, she knew, were for him and for herself.

She swung her arm forward indicating the chairs, and Ken grabbed two in each hand and followed her back up the stairs. *You're a special lady* rang in her ears long after she'd made her way into the living room.

"Thank you for coming," she said as she moved among the mourners—kind people who knew her father mainly from knowing her.

Little by little, people began to say goodbye, and she slipped off her shoes and pushed them beneath a lamp table, hoping she'd remember what she'd done with them later. The freedom eased pressure from her toes, and she only wished it would work on her spirit. Before she stepped away, a hand rested on her arm.

"Annie, I want to extend my sympathy."

She turned to face a shock of long red hair and a warm smile of her ex-employer, Claire, who owned Loving Treasures. "Claire. Thank you for coming."

Claire nodded, her gaze searching Annie's, and she fingered the only exotic thing she'd worn that day, an Indian fetish necklace adorned with miniature carvings of birds and animals. The turquoise, jet and sterling silver wrapped in multiple strands around her sturdy neck.

"I hope you don't mind my asking…about the artwork." She gestured toward one of Annie's small paintings.

"No. I don't mind." She looked at the woman's

expression, trying to imagine what she might ask. "Did you have a question?"

"Are these the paintings Ken talked about with me?"

"Ken?" Annie's mind flew in a multitude of directions. "I don't understand."

"Oh, I'm sorry," Claire said. "Maybe I've ruined a surprise."

Annie shook her head, still not getting the message. "I don't know of any surprise. Did Ken mention my paintings?"

"He did. A few days ago."

"Really?"

Claire nodded and moved closer to two sailboats drifting on a sunset lake. "This is lovely."

"Thank you," Annie said, glancing around the room to see if she could spot Ken so she could speak with him.

"I'd like to see more of these."

Annie opened her mouth to explain today wasn't a good day, but Claire let out a soft chuckle.

"Not today, naturally. Come and see me once you're...when you have time."

"I will," Annie said, lost by the conversation, but too busy to pursue it now.

Claire moved off and Annie's good friends, Philip and Jemma Somerville stepped beside her. Jemma gave Annie a hug while Philip stood nearby, his look concerned.

"We're so sorry," Jemma said. "This puts a big hole in your life, I know."

Annie nodded, clinging to her self-control. Jemma's sad eyes had triggered the reality. Though her father had been more than a handful, Annie's life would never be the same.

Philip took her hand. "We'll be praying for you."

Others moved in to make a quick goodbye, and soon even the few neighbors who had remained to clean up had gone. While Ken returned the chairs to the basement, Annie wandered around the living room finding stray paper cups and napkins, anxious to ask him about her conversation with Claire.

"Sit, Annie," Bill said.

Annie eyed Susan resting in the recliner, and Donna curled in another chair. She looked at her brother standing with his shoulder braced against the doorjamb. To her delight, he opened his arms, and she walked into them, enjoying the first sign of familial love she had experienced. When she drew back, he guided her to the sofa then sat beside her.

"I think it's time we all have a heart-to-heart talk," he said.

# Chapter Seven

Annie's pulse heightened, as she wondered what Bill had to say. She had no question about her sisters' attitudes. They'd made it clear. They wanted their share. Share? The word made her laugh, a sad sort of laugh that hurt in her chest.

Her brother patted Annie's hand as he spoke. "Let's look at it this way. We've all seen the will, and according to what we found, Pa gave us equal shares of the estate."

Susan and Donna nodded, faint smiles on their lips.

"But we all know Pa didn't have much," Bill continued. "That insurance policy doesn't cover the funeral, and the little he has in the bank won't make any of us rich."

Susan's expression had shifted from the pleasant one she'd pasted on her face to one of annoyance. "What's the point, Bill?"

"The point is, what's left?" He swung his arm outward. "The house. That's it."

"So?" Donna said. "It must be worth something. The mortgage has been paid off for years."

Bill's amiable mood deflated like a balloon pricked by a pin. "What's it really worth to us? Not much." He rose and paced across the room. "But it's worth everything to Annie." He reached the fireplace and grasped the mantel, his knuckles white. "Do you want to throw our sister out of her home?"

The two woman looked at each other, then back at Bill. Annie's gaze shifted further to Ken, standing in the far doorway, leaning against the jamb.

"We're not throwing her out," Donna said. "It's in Pa's will."

Susan slapped her hand against the chair. "I think fair is fair."

Bill lowered his arm and moved away from the hearth. He plunged his hands into his pockets and rattled the change as he thought. "Ladies, I don't know how to explain this to you if you're both so pigheaded determined."

"Don't call me pigheaded," Susan said, lurching from the chair and strutting toward the doorway.

Ken shifted out of her way as she tore past. He glanced at her over his shoulder, then moved to Annie's side. "I think I'd better leave. This is family business."

"Sit, please." She patted the cushion beside her.

"No, I really—"

"Susan," Bill called. "Please come in here and discuss this like a family."

"Really," Ken whispered, he brushed his fingers against her cheek. "I'll call you later."

Susan's angry voice sputtered from the kitchen, and she marched into the room holding the brandy snifter she'd found earlier—this time filled with liquor.

Annie gave in. Too many voices filled the room, and the earlier silence she had dreaded seemed now like a lost gift. She nodded to Ken as he slipped to the door and vanished.

Her siblings argued back and forth as if she weren't in the room. Finally she had had enough. "Listen to me. Please."

The voices stopped, and three faces turned to her in surprise.

"Yes, I've taken care of our father for the past years. I gave up my job and my own dreams so that none of you had to give up yours…and so we didn't have to put him in a home and share the expenses."

"Annie—"

"Let her finish," Bill said, holding his palm up to Susan. "We've had our say. It's Annie's turn."

"If Pa wanted you to have a share of the house, that's what it will be," Annie said. "We need to talk with the attorney and have an official reading just to see—"

"Maybe he had a secret stash," Donna said.

All eyes turned to her with looks of disbelief.

"I'm sorry," Donna said. "I was only kidding."

"Annie has a point," Bill said. "We should call

the attorney now and see if we can talk with him tomorrow while we're all here. Can you both stay another day?''

Donna shrugged, and while they waited, Susan dug in her purse for her cell phone. She punched in the number and spoke to her husband, then clicked off. ''One more day but that's it.''

''Then let's hope he can see us tomorrow.'' Bill rose and sat beside the telephone. ''Where's a phone book, Annie?''

When Ken pulled in front of Annie's house, she was already bounding down the steps, her purse strung over her arm as if she were waiting for him. Her platinum hair shone in the late-afternoon sun like a halo.

''Thanks for calling,'' she said, pulling open the passenger door before he could think of being a gentleman. She closed it and released a lengthy sigh.

''You're welcome,'' he said, shifting into Drive and pulling away.

Before they reached the corner, Annie leaned back, breathed another sigh, and gave Ken a faint smile.

Seeing her smile sent a comfortable warmth traveling through him. A feeling he hadn't had in days.

''Where's the rest of the family?''

She tilted her head and gazed out the passenger window for a minute before answering. ''Bill went out to dinner with an old friend, and my sisters wanted to go to Bil-Mar's in Grand Haven. I told them I was too tired.''

"You look tired," Ken said.

"I just needed a break." She glanced out the window. "Where are we going?"

"To the city park."

"The park?"

"I thought you'd enjoy the fresh air."

"Fresh air sounds good," she said.

In another minute, he pulled into the small parking lot and turned off the ignition. He grinned at Annie sliding out her door, determined to ruin any hopes of him being a gentleman. He'd never been the door-opening type anyway, but being with Annie, he wanted to open doors—doors of all kinds.

He got out and hit the remote as he walked around the car to Annie's side. They stepped onto the grass and headed for the nearest empty picnic bench.

The air smelled of warm earth and mowed grass mixed with a faint scent of Annie's perfume. Ken drew in a breath, feeling free and relaxed. He wanted to know what had happened after he'd left earlier in the afternoon, but instead, he waited, letting Annie take her time.

They walked in silence, and when they reached the table, Annie sat and stretched her legs along the bench. Leaning forward, she slid her hands down to her ankles and tilted her head, watching him.

"What?" Ken asked, bracing his hands on the table edge, curious to know what was on her mind.

She grinned. "Just thinking."

"I suppose it would cost more than a penny to find out."

Her mouth curved to a bright smile that faded too quickly. "My brother called the attorney today. We have an appointment tomorrow for the reading of the will."

"You're okay with what's going on?" he asked.

She nodded. "You heard Bill, didn't you?"

"A little before I left." He lifted one hand and rubbed his neck, remembering the argument he'd walked out on.

"He's the only one who seems to understand," Annie said.

"He's on your side."

"Seems to be. I'll just have to have faith it'll work out."

Ken figured she needed more than faith, but who was he to doubt? Lately, he didn't know what to think, what to believe. He'd make his judgment tomorrow after they talked with the attorney.

"They shock me, you know." She slid her legs from the bench and straightened.

"Your sisters?"

She nodded. "Pa's been dead a couple of days and they're worried about what they'll get and about hurrying back to their lives."

Tears rose in her eyes while she looked at him. "I don't think they've even wept." She lifted a hand and brushed the moisture from her cheeks.

Ken moved around the table and sat beside her on the bench. "They're different than you are, Annie." He reached over to caress her damp fingers, daunted by her sadness.

She nodded. "I know. I just can't believe it. They're leaving for home after we're finished at the attorney's office. He's in Grand Haven."

"At least by then you'll know what's what."

"Yes. By then I'll know," she repeated.

Ken sat in silence, enjoying the quiet, yet his thoughts were a cacophony of worry, wondering what would really happen tomorrow. A cardinal's song warbled from overhead, and he looked at Annie, her face thoughtful and drawn.

"I know you're worried," he said.

She shook her head. "Yes, but right now I'm thinking about you."

"Me?"

"What you told me yesterday about your family. I feel as if my problems are so unimportant compared to—"

"Annie, that was long ago. I was a kid. I'm over it."

"But you're not," she said. "I've seen it in your eyes. The sadness and pain. I wondered what it meant, but it wasn't my business to ask. To be honest, I was afraid you had some dark secret."

Her words jolted him to the core.

"At least now I understand," she said, sending him a reassuring grin.

Understand? Could she ever understand? The weight of his guilt knocked the wind from him. She didn't know the half of it, and today, looking at her innocent face and hearing her words, he wondered if he could ever tell her the truth.

"The only pain I feel is a little arthritis," he said, trying to lighten the moment and escape dwelling on the issue.

Annie gave him a nudge with her shoulder. "Men. They never want to admit weakness."

She'd spoken some truth there, but Ken let it ride. Nothing he could say could change things.

They slid into silence, and he watched her attention drift toward a stand of birches. Ken rested his elbow on the plank table top and followed the direction of her gaze. A shaft of sunlight cut through the branches, spreading dark and light mosaic on the grass beneath the trees. In the center of the checkered pattern, a cardinal swooped in and landed. Bright red on gold and black. The bird cocked his head, then pecked at something that had caught his eye. The single bright spot in the shadows intrigued Ken...as it seemingly had Annie.

"That would make a lovely painting," she said, turning her attention back to Ken. "One bright moment in a checkered world...like now. I feel good being here with you."

"Me, too," he said. When he moved to grasp her hand, the bird fluttered away and settled in a tree branch overhead. "Sorry, I chased your bird away."

"As long as you don't chase me away," she said.

"I never want to scare you away, Annie. You're as lovely as the setting sun spreading on the horizon, all color and light...like one of your watercolors."

She looked surprised and whispered a quiet thank you. Annie remained silent a moment, then her eyes widened. "Speaking of my watercolors, I've wanted to ask you about something Claire said to me earlier today."

*Claire.* In all the chaos, Ken had forgotten his talk with Claire.

"What was that about?" Annie asked.

"I'm sorry. I'd planned to tell you, but it was the day you called EMS. It just slipped my mind."

"I understand, but what did you talk about?"

He slid his hand along her arm and rested his palm against her soft skin. He didn't tell her about the other stops he'd made that day. Instead he told her the conversation he'd had with Claire. "I should have asked you first, Annie. I seem to have a knack for taking charge of things when they're really not my business."

She lowered her eyes a minute, her expression unreadable. "You don't have to apologize…but I'm not sure what I want to do now. I need to get Pa's affairs settled, and—"

"If I'd known about your father when I spoke to her, I—"

"Stop," she said, placing her other hand over his. "Let's not blow this out of proportion."

He did as she asked, afraid he'd overstepped his bounds, yet enjoying the warmth of her palm against his flesh.

"I'm not upset, Ken. You were kind to ask her. I'm just saying I have other things on my mind now, but when everything's over, I'll give it some thought."

*When everything's over.* The thought skittered through him, leaving an unpleasant chill. Annie had faith. Ken had fear. Tomorrow would tell part of the tale. He'd have to wait and see.

In the attorney's waiting room, Annie sat with her hands clasped in her lap while Susan talked with her husband on the cell phone. Bill paced the floor, jingling keys until Annie wanted to scream. Donna stared at her nails, longing for a manicure, Annie was certain.

Annie's nerves were raw. She'd tried to be civil all morning, and yet Ken's warning filled her head. You can't sit back and let them take away your house. Speak your mind.

She'd done all she could. Last night, she'd prayed harder than she'd prayed in years, asking God to give her direction and to help her deal with whatever happened. The thought of her house being put on the market sent ice slithering through her veins. She'd covered the reality with hope, but her hope was fading. She'd seen the will herself. She just needed to hear it read officially.

A secretary rose and moved toward them. "Mr. Becker is ready to see you now."

Standing in the middle of the room, Bill turned to motion them forward. Annie rose, and Donna followed. Annie paused and waited. Susan sat a moment, saying good-bye, then closed her cell phone and dropped it in her handbag.

They followed Bill like three blind mice, Annie

thought. None of them knowing for sure what was about to happen. As they came through the doorway, Becker was standing beside his desk. He motioned to three chairs lined up in front, then dragged another from the wall to join the others.

After the introductions, Becker began. "First, I'm sorry for your loss. I know losing a parent can be a difficult experience."

His serious expression made Annie wince. If the man could look in the hearts of the four people in front of him, he'd be surprised that most of them felt no loss or deep grief at all. Even Annie, who felt loss, also realized for the first time her freedom. Freedom to do what, she didn't know. But freedom.

"Now, we should get down to business," Becker said, lowering himself to his executive chair. He pulled a file folder forward and flipped open the cover.

"As the executor of your father's estate, I'm sorry to say he has very little. His extended illness has cut into his bank account. Instead of insurance, I suggested he invest some money in annuities. Though he hasn't invested in the fund in years, it has accrued some interest."

Stress eased from her siblings face while Annie frowned in surprise. "Annuities? Pa never mentioned any investment."

"He invested years ago. He'd probably forgotten," Becker said. "It's not a fortune. About fifty-six thousand now, I'd guess."

"Fifty-six thousand." Annie's sisters said in unison.

"I'm surprised," Bill said.

He wasn't more surprised than Annie, but she didn't respond. While the thought eased her mind, she wondered if the information would only stimulate her sisters' greed.

"And then we have the house," Becker said.

"I wonder what that's worth," Donna said.

"We'll know soon enough," Susan muttered.

"Now to the will." Becker shifted the documents in front of him.

"We have a copy of it here," Bill said. He leaned forward and extended the papers toward Becker.

Becker frowned and took the paper from Bill's hand. Unfolding it, he studied it for a moment, then refolded it and handed it back to Bill. The attorney lifted his head and let his gaze travel over the four of them. "Your father has added a codicil to his will."

"A codicil," Donna said.

"When did he do that?" Susan asked.

"Following your mother's death," Becker said.

Bill's gaze caught Annie's. A relieved look washed over his face, but Annie wasn't that hopeful.

Susan's face paled. "How does that change things?"

Annie held her breath, wondering the same thing.

# Chapter Eight

Outside the attorney's office, Annie stood beside Bill watching their sisters climb into the car. Their scowls had eased. The knowledge they were ten thousand dollars richer seemed to take away the initial sting of the will's codicil.

As the car pulled away, Bill rested his hand on Annie's shoulder and gave it a squeeze. "You deserve the house. Don't let Susan or Donna make you feel guilty. Pa did the right thing for once."

She watched the wavy shimmer of heat rise from the pavement and nodded. "Thanks, Bill."

Before she could say more, a taxi pulled up beside them.

"Here's my ride," her brother said. "Time to catch a plane."

"I don't know why you didn't let me drive you to the airport."

"You need a break, Annie. Get some rest." He

handed his overnight bag to the driver, then clasped Annie's shoulders. "I love you, sis. If you need anything, you call." He kissed her cheek, then turned and slid into the cab.

When the driver slammed the door, Annie watched him through the window as nostalgia washed over her. Memories of their childhood skittered through her mind. Bill had been the one who'd always been the peacemaker. *Blessed are the peacemakers.* She closed her eyes, thanking God for standing by her side.

Hearing a door close, Annie opened her eyes and saw Ken standing beside his truck. Her heart kicked into high gear. "What are you doing here?" she asked when he neared.

"Worried about you." His square chin with the deep cleft set against his craggy jaw appeared tense and determined. "How did it go?"

"Good."

"Good?"

"Much better than I expected."

"The house?"

"Mine," she said. "Pa had a codicil to the original will."

Tension eased in his serious face. "Then it's over."

She shrugged. "You never know with my sisters, but I hope so. Pa had an annuity none of us knew about so after we pay off the attorney fees and the funeral costs, everyone will get ten thousand or so."

He stared at his foot, shifting a pebble back and

forth with his toe. ''You were right. That faith you talk about seemed to work.''

''It's not the faith working. God does the work. He came through and answered my prayers.''

He shook his head. ''I admire you, Annie.'' Slipping his arm around her shoulder, he drew her closer and kissed the top of her head. Heat wrapped around her—the sun and her emotions squeezing against her lungs.

Ken eased back. ''Got some time? I'd like to hear the blow by blow.''

Annie looked at her wristwatch. ''Sure. Someplace around here?''

''Not far,'' he said. ''Hop into the truck, and I'll drop you back here for your car later.''

She shrugged. ''Okay.'' He left her feeling curious. They walked to the vehicle in silence, and once inside, Ken cranked up the air conditioning while Annie leaned back and closed her eyes, her mind filled with thought.

Ken snapped on the radio, leaving it low and found a light jazz station. The soft music lulled her until the tension she'd felt earlier melted away.

''Nice choice,'' she said.

''I like jazz…and blues.''

''Me, too.'' She straightened her back and shifted toward him. ''I couldn't believe what happened in there today. You should have seen my sisters when Mr. Becker said Pa had added a codicil to the will after my mother died.''

''That long ago!''

"I know. I was surprised."

They were quiet for a moment, then Ken broke the silence. "One of these days you're going to have to explain things to me."

"Explain what things?"

"About clinging to faith rather than taking action. You could have lost so much." He lifted his gaze to her.

"Faith is hard to explain. It's in here." She rested her fingers against her heart. "Or maybe here."

"In the gut?" He gave her a soft chuckle.

"Um-hum. A little of both I think. You just know what's supposed to happen will happen."

He lifted his hand from the steering wheel and ran his fingers through his hair. "Even when it's wrong?"

"It might seem wrong, but it might not be. God could have other plans for you."

Ken pushed his back against the seat, trying to comprehend what she'd said. Was she gullible...or was that really faith? Faith seemed to involve acceptance. Finding approval for whatever happened in life even when it seemed wrong or unfair. Faith intimated a forgiving God. A God who didn't punish, but forgave.

As always, his thoughts fell into the darkness. How could anyone think what happened to him had been right or fair?

"You don't understand?" Annie asked.

"I'm a hopeless case, Annie."

"No you're not. You're just a slow learner."

They both laughed and to Ken, it felt good. He

turned down the next street and pulled into his driveway.

"Where are we?" Annie asked.

"My house. You've never been here before."

"Your house?"

"Right." He motioned to the bungalow. "That's a house. Walls, roof, doors, windows. Now who's the slow learner?"

Annie chuckled and pushed opened her door.

Loving to hear her laugh, Ken jumped out and darted around the car to help her with the long step down. He grinned when he made it before she alighted. "You're a hard woman to show manners to. You never let me be a gentleman."

"You are a gentleman. In every way. You don't need to open doors to prove that."

Ken motioned Annie up the steps to the small porch while he found the key. He opened the door and ushered her inside, then closed it against the heat. "This is it," he said, gesturing toward the archway.

Annie stopped in the living-room threshold, her gaze shifting from one side of the room to the other. "You have a nice place. Masculine, yet cozy."

"Thanks." He chuckled, never thinking of his furniture that he'd shoved into the room as masculine or cozy. But it met his needs—a place he could prop his feet with a good light so he could read a book or scan the newspaper. A small TV for lonely nights and a good CD player for music.

*Music hath charms to soothe the savage breast.* The quotation settled over him. After he'd left prison, he'd thought of himself as some kind of savage...something less than human. At least that thought had faded.

Ken pulled himself from his memories. "Want a tour of the mansion?"

"Sure," she said, following him into the kitchen. She paused and scanned the room. "Small, like mine, but nice."

"It works for my culinary arts. Doesn't take much to tear open a bag of chips and make a sandwich."

She grinned and crossed the room to the back window. Pushing aside the curtain, she rested her hands on the sill. "Ken, it's lovely." She glanced at him over her shoulder, a grin glowing on her face. "Who's your landscaper?"

"You wouldn't like him," Ken said, grinning back. He crossed the floor to stand behind her. "Would you like a tour outside?"

"I would," she said, reaching for the knob.

She stepped onto the small stoop, and he followed her to the lawn.

The sun swathed his cooler skin, but didn't warm him as much as seeing Annie smiling and more relaxed than she'd been in days.

She spun around to face him. "Let's do this to my yard, with some new flower beds and a bird bath. Maybe a couple of flowering shrubs."

"Sure. Your landscaper will appreciate your business." He grasped her arms from behind and drew her closer as he looked at the yard. The fragrance of citrus and sunshine rose from her shining hair. He clung to her arms to control the desire to kiss her cream-colored neck, so tempting beneath the knot of gold.

Annie wriggled from his grasp and turned to face him—so close he could feel the warmth of her breath. As if realizing they were nose to nose, she eased away. "Let's plan some flower beds, really."

"You should. It's your house now." The words slipped over him like a peaceful river.

She nodded. "It feels so good to know it's mine."

Hers. Imagining Annie having to sell the house had gnawed at him like a mouse on cheese. The vision had torn away chunks of his patience and forgiveness. With that problem solved, he found himself hopeful again. Hopeful that Annie would find a new life. A new life with...

With who? With him? The thought knifed through him. After Cheryl, he'd made a vow to live a quiet life, to stick to himself, never to admit his prison record. By getting tangled in Annie's life, he'd broken his own promise.

"Why so quiet?" Annie asked.

"Thinking...about you."

"Me?"

"You," he said, taking her hand and guiding her back inside. The cool air settled over him again as he steered her toward the living room.

When she settled on the sofa, her expression had changed, and she looked serious. "I've been thinking, too, about what you asked."

"What did I ask?"

"How I can accept God's will and why I have such strong faith."

"And suddenly you have an answer?"

She grinned. "It's in the Bible. You don't happen to have one, do you?"

"Sorry. No. I…" An image shot into his mind. In the bottom drawer in the spare bedroom, he'd kept some of his mother's belongings. He recalled a small leather-bound book. His mother's Bible, so different from the heavy black leather one that had stung his face and pounded his back.

"Just a minute," he said, rising from the table. His pulse charged as he made his way down the short hall to the back bedroom. He bent and pulled open a dresser drawer. Shifting things around, he sorted through the items until his fingers wrapped around the red book, smaller than a paperback, but covered in leather with gold-embossed words, *New Testament.*

He carried it back to the kitchen, wondering if this is what she wanted. As he came through the doorway, he held it up. "Bible?"

"Part of the Bible," she said.

She held out her hand and he placed his mother's book into it. "It looks old. My mom had one of these given to her in elementary school. I remember her showing it to me. It's the King James Version."

His father had read from the King James. He remembered the thees and thous, the knoweths and sayeths that had made his bones shudder. He waited, listening to the soft crinkle sound as Annie flipped through the thin pages.

She stopped.

"Here," she said, catching his gaze. "Listen to this. *'And this is the confidence that we have in him, that, if we ask any thing according to his will, he heareth us: And if we know that he hear us, whatsoever we ask, we know that we have the petitions that we desired of him.'"* She lifted her gaze from the page.

"Those heareths lost me," Ken said, trying to make a joke to cover his anxiety.

"It's clearer in one of the more modern versions. It means we can be confident that God hears our prayers when we ask for things that are His will."

Ken rested his elbows on his knees. "See, there's the catch. They have to be God's will, not ours."

"But if we believe, then God's will is our will."

Ken shook his head. He was sure it made sense to Annie, but it still seemed vague to him.

"You'll have to read this for yourself." She laid the book on the table and gave it a pat.

He stared at the small volume, questioning whether it really had something for him inside its pages.

"You could go to church with me on Sunday. That would be a beginning." She gave him a hopeful look.

He hated to disappoint her, but he shook his head. Somehow, churches seemed to make him feel even more sinful. Annie was so pure. His mind spun with awareness. He wasn't being fair to her. He couldn't tell her the truth, and if he couldn't, he needed to let her go.

*   *   *

Sitting in her living room, Annie listened to the silence. She'd prayed for quiet while her sisters were visiting, but now that they were gone, the past week had settled around her like a scratchy woolen blanket—stifling and confining.

Ken had called when he could, but he'd gotten back to his regular work schedule, and he'd been working long hours to catch up. Still, she worried now that her problems had been settled, whether she'd upset him with the discussion about God or the invitation to church. Or maybe now that he'd done his kind deed, his compassion would head in some other direction.

Silly. The answer could be either, but more likely the June sunshine had done its work and kept Ken busy. Her own bushes were sprouting new limbs heading off in unwieldy directions. A landscaper's work grew busy now that people wanted new shrubs and flowers. Everyone in town stood outside their homes with shovels or clippers, planting and pruning. Landscaping was Ken's business.

Annie thought about the flower beds. She'd sketched out some crude plans of what she might like in her yard. New landscape meant Ken would spend more time with her. She hated scheming, but the idea pushed her on.

When she rose to find the childlike drawings, her gaze traveled to her artwork and she remembered Claire's invitation to show her more of her artwork. Though the offer was kind, the idea hadn't settled well in her imagination. She liked the paintings, but they were hers. Would someone else find them attractive enough to pay money for them? Searching the attic hardly seemed worth the effort.

Instead, Annie scanned the living room. She eyed the heavy draperies and the dark overstuffed furniture. Since the house was now hers, refurbishing it sounded more practical. With the extra money her father had left her, she could pay tribute to him by making the house a home.

She liked the idea and rose to find a notepad so she could make a list of things she wanted to do. She found the paper, but before starting, sounds from outside drew her to the window.

Ken's truck sat in front of the house, and she watched him walk to the bed and pull out his equipment. Her pulse skittered as she watched him stride up the driveway toward the backyard. She longed to run outside, but she couldn't do that. He'd been a good friend when she needed one. That was it.

Hating the rush of mixed emotion, she sank into the sofa cushion, trying to concentrate on what she'd like to do with the room. This room, of all of them, seemed ponderous and repressive. It needed light. Pull down the draperies, she thought. She could get rid of the dark mahogany furniture and find a new sofa and chair in pastel shades. Something to brighten her life the way her paintings did to the one wall.

Her hand tensed as she jotted ideas, and finally, she put the pen and notepad on the table, unable to collect her thoughts.

Making her way to the kitchen, she watched Ken through the window as he headed back to the front yard. She leaned back against the counter, bound in thought.

He'd become too important to her. Not just as a friend, but more than that. She'd felt her heartstrings wrap around him. Though he still seemed reserved and private in many ways, he'd given her so much in the past weeks with his sweet…loving ways.

Ken would deny it if she told him.

Her heart skipped a beat when she heard a knock at the door. She hurried into the living room and saw him standing there in a faded T-shirt and jeans.

"Ken. How are you?" She pushed open the screen door.

He didn't move. "The question is, how are you?"

Stress filled his face as if he'd spent many sleepless nights, and Annie wondered what was wrong. "Are you ill?"

"Just busy. I let things slide when your father died. I'm trying to catch up."

She wanted to thank him for all he'd done, but she knew he would only brush off his kindness.

He hesitated, rocking on his heels, the cleft in his chin deepening with his serious look. "I'm sorry I've been so busy. How have you been?"

"Lonely."

As if taking a deep breath, he lifted his shoulders. "It has been." His gaze captured hers.

Annie pushed the door open farther and stood back, leaving the opening wide. "Can you come in for a minute?"

"For a minute." He caught the door as Annie

moved ahead of him, and he followed her to the living room.

"You look hot and tired. I'll get you some iced tea," she said, stepping toward the kitchen before he could say no.

She grabbed a tumbler, dropped in some ice and filled it with the drink. When she turned around, Ken stood beside her so close she could smell the heat of his skin. His unexpected appearance startled her, and she jumped. Liquid sloshed from the glass to her hand.

"Sorry. I didn't know you'd followed me," she said, handing him the glass and grabbing a napkin.

The look in his eye made her nervous. It was a look she'd never seen before. One that made her feel feminine and desired.

He set the glass on the counter and drew her into his arms. "I didn't want to, Annie, but I've missed you." His voice sounded husky and unsteady.

"I missed you, too," she whispered.

She saw his mouth moving toward hers, as slow as a bud opening in the sun. Surprised yet happy, she prepared herself as his warm, soft mouth covered hers, taking away her breath, but filling her with life. Slow and tender, his kiss was a caress she'd enjoyed in dreams.

He eased back, searching her eyes as if to ask if he'd been wrong to kiss her.

How could it be wrong?

He let his fingers linger along her jaw and brush

away a few strands of hair that had strayed onto her cheek. "I'm fighting this, but I'm losing the battle."

She wanted to cry out. *Lose! Lose!* But she sensed she might scare him. Something so deep…something so dark and deep dwelled inside him. It seemed more than his upbringing. More than an angry father. She sensed it. If only she knew what hurt or shame or guilt tore at his soul. If he'd only give the burden to God.

"We're not at war, Ken. You have no battle to win or lose. We're two people who enjoy each other's company. Nothing more or less. Sometimes it's nice to feel the heartbeat of another human being."

Where the words came from, Annie didn't know, but they seemed to touch a cord. Ken's face eased, and he brushed his hair back with a nod.

"I'm making too much of it, I guess." He lifted the glass and took a drink. "I don't want to hurt you, Annie."

"You'd never hurt me on purpose. I know that." But the sound of his voice sent a shiver coursing along her spine. Enough, she thought. Mountains from mole hills.

She grasped his arm. "Now, let's not be so serious. Come into the living room, I want to show you the sketches I made for the garden, and then I want you to help me make some decisions."

"Decisions?"

"I'm planning some changes."

A curious scowl moved to his face.

"I'm going to buy some new furniture and brighten up the house."

"Brighten things up," he said, following her through the doorway. "Making changes?"

"A few," she said.

He stood in the doorway, his craggy face rutted with stress. "We can all use some changes."

# Chapter Nine

Ken did a full turn, eyeing the changes in Annie's living room. Not a lot yet, but some. She'd pulled down the draperies and now lacy curtains hung at the windows, allowing light to spread across the worn carpet. He'd tried to do the same—not with his home, but with his outlook.

"What do you think?" Annie asked.

"It's different," he said.

"It'll be even more different when the furniture's delivered."

He nodded, not sure how comfortable he felt with the change. He'd told her to get a life. And that's what she was doing, but now a strange sensation crept in. Annie would blossom in the sunlight while he cowered in the darkness. The image startled him. Foolish. Annie had only bought new furniture.

Fear of losing her pierced his thoughts. Yet how could he lose something he didn't have, and something he could never have? If only he could enjoy the friendship and let it go at that, but his emotions had gotten involved—emotions he'd thought had atrophied to a nub. They'd roused and sometimes felt as if they'd burst inside him. He couldn't deal with feelings. Years ago he'd had enough of them for a lifetime.

"It'll be nice," he said.

"I've decided to look in the attic for a couple of my paintings. I could use something over the sofa. Something brighter."

Her comment reminded him. "Have you talked with Claire?"

She shook her head.

He wanted to ask her why not, but he closed his mouth and let it drop. She would in her own good time.

"Want to help?" she asked.

"Help?"

"Look for the pictures." She tilted her head, waiting for his answer.

"Sure," he said, "but not now. I have two more jobs to finish. Tonight maybe?"

She shrugged a shoulder. "Can't. Tonight I'm babysitting for Jemma Somerville. She's bringing Ellie over about seven o'clock."

"Maybe another time then."

"Tomorrow evening would be fine," Annie said. "And if you'd like, drop by later. You can play with the blocks."

Play with blocks. Her enthusiasm made him grin.

"I'll see how it goes." He glanced at his watch. "I'd better get."

She nodded and walked him to the door.

He descended the porch steps and gave her a wave.

Blocks. He couldn't even imagine.

Ellie stretched her baby arms toward Annie. She held a picture book clutched in her fingers.

Annie bent down and lifted the child. The softness of the one-year-old's skin aroused Annie's senses. She'd never hold her own child. Never hear the cooing of her own little one. Never see the child's plump legs kicking or its flailing arms reaching for her.

She sloughed off the emotion and cuddled Ellie to her chest. "Let's go outside and look at the book."

What she'd longed to do all day was gather a bouquet from her small garden, but she'd been too busy, too distracted. She'd noticed earlier some cone flowers and coreopsis had bloomed, and she pictured a vase filled with them to brighten her living room. She hadn't given Ken her garden sketches either. She had a million ideas. She wanted changes. Changes in her surroundings. Changes in her life.

But not with a toddler at her side.

Annie opened the door, breathing in the mid-June evening air. Though the hour was after seven, the sun was far from setting and the diffuse light made this time of day soft and cheery.

Scooting a puzzle and wooden building blocks from her path, Annie made her way to the swing. Ellie grinned as they settled on the seat, and the squeak of the old chains sent her mind back millions of years, it seemed, rather than only weeks ago when Ken had volunteered to oil them.

She placed Ellie on her lap and opened the book, flipping through the pages while the happy child pointed and cooed at the pictures. When she closed the cover, Ellie squirmed from her lap and picked up a puzzle. The pieces Annie had just put back together fell one by one to the planks.

Annie smiled and shook her head. "One more time, Ellie. Then it's almost bedtime."

At the word *bed,* Ellie whined, her bottom lip extended like a shelf.

Annie ignored the pout and joined her on the floor. While she turned the pieces upright, the toddler tried to force the large cardboard shapes into the frame.

"Annie?" Ken's voice sailed over the porch half wall.

"I'm here," she called.

Ken came up the stairs and stopped, amazed at the vision—two blond heads bent over a child's puzzle. Annie looked up, her face flushed and smiling.

"Hi," she said. "This is Ellie."

"Hello, Ellie," Ken said, mesmerized by the vision he saw.

Ellie grasped the edge of the jigsaw puzzle and lifted it toward him before Annie could stop her.

"Ellie…" Annie shook her head, watching the pieces fall to the floor.

Ken grinned, marveling at the joy in Annie's face. The child's grin brought one to his own.

Annie rose and motioned for Ken to take her place. "Your turn."

Ken gave her a look of panic. He'd never played with a child before, especially not one so young.

"Keep her busy a few minutes. Okay?"

Before letting him answer, Annie swooped through the doorway leaving him stranded with a one-year-old.

Ellie held up a piece, then handed it to Ken.

"You want me to do the puzzle." Ken eyed the child, her face so honest and trusting.

He knelt beside her and picked up a piece from the floor, bending it this way and that until it finally slid into the right spot. Ken chuckled.

As they finished placing the last puzzle piece, Annie's voice came through the screen door.

"When you're finished, bring her inside."

Ken stared at Ellie wondering what to do. Leaving the child on the floor, he straightened his kinked legs, understanding why Annie had sat on the wooden planks. Age didn't play kindly with tired limbs.

Ellie saw him stand and pushed her stubby legs upward with her hands pressed against the floor. Ken reached out his hand and she grasped his finger, toddling on wobbly legs through the front door.

Inside, Annie stood at the kitchen sink, filling a vase with water. A colorful bouquet lay on the counter, and she turned and grinned. "Flowers. I've been wanting to do this all day since I noticed they were blooming."

Ellie lifted both hands, making fists toward the blossoms.

"Want a flower?" Annie asked. She plucked a stem from the counter and handed it to the child.

Ken watched her patience as the little girl clung to Annie's pant leg as if she thought she could climb up to get in on the action.

Annie arranged one more bloom, then gazed down at the child. "I suppose you want to help." She gave Ken a hopeless grin, then leaned down and kissed Ellie's cheek. "You can help for a minute, sweetie, then it's time for bed."

Ken watched while Ellie stuck out her lower lip, but Annie just ignored it and tickled the child until she broke out in giggles. So did Annie.

Seeing her with the child touched Ken's heart. He longed to take Annie in his arms as he'd done earlier that day and kiss her glowing cheeks. She was meant to be a mother. The thought twisted his joy to sadness.

Annie would say being without a child of her own was God's will.

How could a loving God cheat a beautiful woman of her greatest joy?

In the glare of the unshaded bulb, Annie shifted cartons and trunks from the gloomy recesses of the attic. "Here's a couple more," she said, bringing out two paintings wrapped in butcher paper.

She handed Ken the paintings, then plowed back into the jumble of furniture and boxed treasures.

Ken sat on an antique chair, the cane seat sagging

so deep he feared putting his full weight on it. He'd balanced two paintings against the chair leg. Now he added two more.

Curious, he wanted to tear away the paper to see the artwork, but Annie had suggested carrying them downstairs and looking at them there.

"Could you help me?" she asked, bending over a crate on the far side of the loft.

Ken rose and made his way around a stack of boxes and an old birdcage. "What's this?"

"It's a crate of watercolors. Ones like I have downstairs."

He looked into the wooden crate, surprised at the number of paintings stored there—some framed, some unframed, but all the same unique style he'd seen on Annie's living-room walls.

"I suppose this is enough for now," she said.

"You mean you have more?"

She shrugged. "Somewhere."

While she carried the four larger paintings, he hoisted the crate into his arms and descended the stairs.

The late-afternoon sun seemed to shine brighter after the attic gloom. He set the paintings on the living-room floor, then looked at Annie, anxious to see her artwork.

Just as he'd expected, as he peeled away the brown paper, Annie's pictures came to life. Seascapes, a butterfly hovering over a summer garden, a chickadee on a thistle, a white, dew-tipped rose, the old Loving lighthouse in winter. Even the smallest watercolor danced with a simple magic.

"These are great," he said.

"I wouldn't say great."

"I would, and so would anyone who saw them. Now that you have these handy, you really should visit Claire and see what she has to say."

Annie gave him a faint smile. "Maybe. When I'm finished decorating."

"You're as stubborn as a child," he said. The word *child* nudged his memory of Ellie.

"Why, thank you," she said, giving him a playful scowl.

"Speaking of children, I had fun watching you with Ellie the other day."

"Did I look frustrated?"

"No. You looked like a mother."

"A grandmother." Her stomach tightened.

"Maternal, then," he said, sensing he'd better compromise.

Sadness washed over Annie, and she shook her head. "You shouldn't start on that."

"Start on what?"

"Talking about motherhood. We both know I missed out on that."

Ken's face darkened. "I didn't mean to make you feel bad. And that's not true. Women are mothers into their forties."

"That's unlikely." The words stabbed her.

"You could enjoy children—like Ellie—and never

be a mother. Some mothers are so rotten they should never have children.''

She studied him. Had his mother been so rotten she should never have had children? Could that be the deep hurt she witnessed in his eyes?

''I realize that,'' she said, ''but now that my dad's gone, reality's reared its head.''

''When I said I had fun watching you with Ellie, I meant it as a compliment.''

''I know you did. I'm sorry. Since Pa died, I...I just don't know. I'm a little edgy, like a fish out of water.''

''What about the paintings?''

''That's a hobby. I enjoy painting, but it's not like a real purpose.''

''You could still be a wife, Annie.''

As the words exited his mouth, Ken seemed to flinch.

His reaction squeezed Annie's heart and shook her with an old reality. This man had no intention of making anyone his wife. She couldn't respond as she watched her fantasy dissipate like a wisp of smoke.

Struggling to keep herself focused, something Jemma had said shot into her mind. ''When Jemma picked up Ellie the other day, she mentioned the owner of the child-care facility where Ellie stays a couple days a week is looking for someone.''

''That would be perfect,'' Ken said. ''You'd have a job and a purpose.''

But not the purpose she wanted. Being a child-care

worker? Could that ever equal being a wife and a mother? She drew in a ragged breath.

Maybe it didn't have to.

Ken stood in the shadow of the fieldstone church. Its square bell tower rose above the shingled roof, while the bells' resonating clang tolled the time for worship.

The bells stopped, and as the tone still echoed on the morning air, Ken heard the organ's pipes through the double doors that stood open like a warm greeting.

But instead of feeling welcome, Ken struggled to get his feet to move forward. Long-bottled hurt popped into his thoughts from the ocean of his memory. He'd corked the bottle long ago. Now, by coming here, he'd opened it again.

Why was he here? For Annie. For the little he could give her. Friendship and company. He'd tried to salve his guilt with the thought. Church was important to her, and she was important to him. So here he was with no promises.

Without Annie's knowledge, Ken climbed the four broad steps and forced himself inside. The entrance led into the sanctuary, and he stood a moment while voices lifted in song. Hoping to go unnoticed, he slid into a back pew and listened to the music.

His mind wandered, asking if Annie was the only reason he'd come to church after all these years. Curiosity? Faith? Hope? He'd had so little these past years.

Hope seemed like a child waiting for Santa. A myth

that would one day have to be explained away. He remembered when he'd learned the jolly old man with the red suit was nothing more than his father, who gave him stones instead of oranges. A father who was far from jolly. Ken had been disillusioned.

The scripture Annie had read slipped through his mind. The words had awakened him. Made him wonder. Made him want to learn more. To understand.

A rustle of noise drew him back, and as the congregation settled in their seats, he followed. In a moment, a minister stepped forward and his voice filled the large church as he read from the Bible—from Romans, he announced. Ken listened to the story of Abraham, an old man, to whom God had made a promise that his elderly wife would give birth to a child.

*Yet he did not waver through unbelief regarding the promise of God, but was strengthened in his faith and gave glory to God, being fully persuaded that God had power to do what he had promised.*

Ken stared at his hands, wondering how an old man and woman could believe that God would give them a child. The idea seemed unfathomable. What would it take to believe? Obviously faith. Complete faith. Annie's kind of faith.

After the reading, the choir rose. Their spirited hymn rang, and he observed looks of joy on people's faces. If only he could find that happiness.

He stretched his neck to see if Annie was there. Near the front, he caught the glint of her platinum hair in the light from an open window.

When the sermon began, Ken thought about sliding back out the door, but hearing a reference to Romans again, he waited, intrigued by the faith of Abraham and Sarah.

The speaker's voice sailed toward him. The words smacked him between the eyes.

*What if some did not have faith? Will their lack of faith nullify God's faithfulness? Not at all! Let God be true, and every man a liar.*

Ken tossed the words about in his mind. Even if he had no faith, God continued to be faithful. Could that be true? Was he the liar mentioned in the verse? While he denied God's promise and his personal faith, had God still remained faithful to him?

Struggling to understand, Ken heard the clergyman's amen. The congregation rose, and Ken stood, too, hoping to slip out the door, but an usher stood in front of it, his hands folded in prayer, his eyes closed. Unwilling to disturb the man, Ken waited. The last hymn followed, and before he realized, people had begun to move from their seats and work their way down the aisle.

Ken stepped into the entrance hall as a hand grasped his sleeve.

"Ken Dewitt, how nice to see you here."

He turned toward the voice and faced Claire. "Thanks. I—"

"Ken."

Annie's voice halted his stumbling explanation. He turned, trying to cover the discomfort that knotted in his throat. "Hi."

"I'm surprised," Annie said, her expression looking pleased, but bewildered.

"So am I." He could think of nothing else as honest.

"Annie, I'm still waiting for your visit," Claire said. "Ken aroused my curiosity and so did the paintings that I saw at your house."

"One of these days, Claire. Soon. Thanks."

Claire nodded and sailed off.

"I guess I'll have to take some paintings over to her shop," Annie said, watching Claire meander among her church friends.

Ken shrugged and took a step backward, wanting to escape. Before he could move, one of his customers grabbed his hand with a firm shake while another called his name from the distance and gave him a wave.

Surrounded by people he knew, Ken felt pinned to the spot, especially since Annie stayed close to his side.

"Annie. There you are."

Annie turned and opened her arms. "Jemma." She gave the woman a warm hug.

Ken looked at Ellie teetering beside her mother. He gave the child a wink, and the baby grinned back. When Ellie lifted her arms to Ken, he faltered.

"Is she flirting with you?" Jemma asked, grinning down at her daughter.

"Ken and Ellie played with some puzzles the other day," Annie said. "You know Ken Dewitt, don't you?"

"Certainly," Jemma said. "He does our landscaping at the house. Anyway, Philip and I are having a few friends over for a Fourth of July barbecue today. Philip has his Bay Breeze Resort employee party tonight, but we had this spur-of-the-moment idea for our friends. I hope you can come." Her gaze shifted from Annie to Ken.

"That sounds fun," Annie said. "How about it?" She eyed Ken.

Ken couldn't avoid her gaze. He felt trapped, pleased to be asked, but caught in a social web he usually avoided.

"We'd love to have you," Jemma said.

Ken gave Jemma a polite smile. "I'm not sure—"

Ellie reached toward Ken, stopping him in mid sentence.

"Maybe you can resist me," Annie said, "but I doubt if you can refuse this young lady." Though she smiled, he watched a measure of disappointment shadow her face.

Annie lifted Ellie into her arms and planted a kiss on her cheek.

The fear of uncertainty, of crowds, of exposure trapped him, but seeing Annie's face changed his mind. "I suppose I can't refuse her."

Annie lowered Ellie to the ground and gave her a pat.

"Great," Jemma said. "We'll see you both about three." She moved off with Ellie toddling at her side.

"I'm sorry. You felt cornered, I know," Annie said.

"No," Ken said, amazed that she'd read his mind. "I really felt as if I were in the way. She's inviting church people."

"So tell me," Annie said, her eyes wide with curiosity. "What are you doing here?"

Ken drew in a shallow breath, asking himself the same question.

# Chapter Ten

At the barbecue, Annie sensed Ken's discomfort. He stood at the sidelines, letting the party happen around him. She longed to know what had brought the dark look to his eyes.

She left the group of women chatting about children and recipes and moved to Ken's side. She noticed his empty hands. "Nothing to drink?"

He slipped his hands in his pockets and shrugged. "Maybe later."

"Okay." She stood with him in silence, wishing she could help him relax. Before she had any idea what she could do, Annie looked up and saw Jemma heading their way.

"Welcome," Jemma said to Ken. "You'll find sodas in the plastic cooler over there." She motioned toward it. "And thermoses of iced tea."

"I'm fine," Ken said. "I'll have something later."

"Great. You know where it is." Jemma's attention

shifted to Annie. "Christie Hanuman just arrived."
She looked away, scanning the guests. "I'll flag her
over and have her meet you."

"Christie Hanuman?" Annie asked, not sure she'd
heard the name before.

"She owns Loving Care. The daycare center."
Jemma's gaze shifted to Ken. "Don't you think the
facility would be a perfect place for Annie to work?"

"If it's what she wants," he said, staying noncommittal.

Annie recalled only days earlier that Ken had
thought it a good idea. Today his reticent reaction
made her curious. Often Ken seemed a puzzle. Not
just any puzzle. With most, a person could unscram-
ble the pieces and find the answer. But Ken's pieces
were tangled and some seemed lost.

Then it struck her. More than likely he wanted her
to put all her effort into the artwork. Ken had defi-
nitely been disappointed she hadn't contacted Claire.
He'd mentioned it numerous times, and she deduced
he was disheartened by her lack of action.

Jemma's face brightened as she lifted a hand, waving at an attractive young woman, perhaps in her early
thirties. "Christie."

"Hi," the woman said as she approached Jemma.
"Thanks for inviting me."

"I'd like you to meet Annie O'Keefe and another
friend, Ken Dewitt."

"Nice to meet you," Christie said, grasping each
of their hands in a firm shake.

Annie listened as Jemma spoke of Christie's child-care facility and mentioned Annie was looking for work. While they talked, Annie noticed Ken had shifted out of the small circle, and she found her mind half on the conversation and half on Ken.

"In fact, I was telling Annie you were looking for help," Jemma said, grabbing Annie's attention.

"Yes, I am," Christie said.

Jemma nudged Annie. "You might be interested, right?"

"I need a job and I like kids," Annie said, embarrassed by Jemma's persistence.

"Stop by next week and fill out an application," Christie said. "I could use someone mature like you."

"If you need a reference, I'll give her one," Jemma said. "When she watches Ellie, I never worry. And Ellie loves her."

Tossing off her funky moment, Annie chuckled. "Jemma's my walking referral."

"Can't go wrong with that," Christie said. "Please come by. Anytime."

"Thanks. Maybe I will," Annie said, her gaze drifting toward Ken, but when she looked around, her spirit lifted. She caught sight of Ken standing beside Philip, helping him keep an eye on the grill. As she watched, Philip gave Ken the barbecue fork while he bent over an ice chest.

When Christie changed to a new topic, Annie excused herself and made her way to Ken's side.

"As I said, I'm pleased with what you've done at

our place," Philip said. "When I have time, we can talk about adding some new shrubbery."

Ken shifted a steak. "Thanks. Sounds good."

"If you ever think about giving up your business, I'd love to hire you at Bay Breeze. I'm about ready to sack my landscaper."

"Thanks, but I like working for myself."

"Can't blame you," Philip said, bending to pull steak from the chest.

"Smells good," Annie said, eyeing the small, plump filets.

Philip nodded. "One of the advantages of owning a resort with a restaurant."

Annie could only imagine. She watched Ken a moment, as he shifted the steaks to the warmer and decorated the top of each with a ruffle-topped toothpick. "What are you doing?"

"Medium rare."

"You're quite the connoisseur," she said.

He chuckled for the first time that day. "No credit here. Philip told me they were ready."

She grinned, pleased to see Ken lighten up and look more genial. Philip greeted another couple who had joined them, then turned to Annie and Ken. "This is Ian and Esther Barry. Ian's my assistant manager at Bay Breeze."

"I've been the head librarian at the Loving Library," Esther said, touching her rounded belly, "but after the baby, I'm not sure." She sent Ian a sheepish grin.

He put his arm around his wife's shoulder. "I think she'll just be a mother…for a while."

She nodded in agreement.

A twinge of envy washed over Annie. For some reason today, a kind of melancholy sat against her chest. She eyed Ian and Esther, looking so happy awaiting the birth of their child, and her gaze drifted to Ken. Again the dark look wavered in his eyes and left her puzzled.

"I think we're about ready," Philip said, signaling to Jemma. "You all should find a seat so we can say the blessing. It's just about time."

"What do you say?" Ken asked, moving to Annie's side.

Annie agreed, and they walked across the lawn to the empty side of a picnic table, greeted a couple from church, and waited for Philip to offer the prayer. When Philip had finished, another man joined them, and after introducing himself as Gordon Henley, he leaned closer toward Ken as if studying his face. "Ken Dewitt?"

Ken nodded, his expression cordial, but Annie felt him tense.

"Sounds familiar," Gordon said, his eyes narrowing.

"I own a landscape service. You've probably seen the name on my truck."

"Maybe, but did you ever live in Cadillac?"

Ken's feet fidgeted beneath the table, and Annie looked at his face, watching anxiety darken his eyes.

He hesitated before answering. "When I was a kid."

"I thought so. We were in third grade together at Roosevelt Elementary. Remember?"

Ken shook his head. "No. I'm sorry."

"Gordon Henley doesn't ring a bell?" the man asked.

Panic rose on Ken's face, and Annie wished she could do something to halt the conversation. Her mind raced, longing to know what this was about and what she could do to make it better.

"No," Ken said. "I have a rotten memory."

"You threatened to punch my lights out."

"Punch your lights out?" Annie said, unable to control her surprise. Ken punching anyone's lights out seemed bizarre.

He grabbed Ken's arm and gave it a shake. "This man was a holy terror in school. I could tell you stories."

"You?" Annie asked, trying to sound lighthearted.

"If the man says so," Ken said as if trying to slough off the comment.

"My family moved in fifth grade—I think it was fifth—so that was the last I saw you. Looks like you're a changed man," Gordon said. "Must be, since you're sitting here surrounded by Christians."

The strain relaxed in Ken's jaw, and he lifted the soda and took a long drink without responding.

The conversation shifted, but Annie's thoughts dwelt on the man's comments. An alien fear settled against her stomach, and she'd lost her appetite, even for a medium-rare filet.

Ken climbed from the truck and headed around the back. As he unloaded his trimmer, Philip came from the house and walked toward his car, jingling his key.

Giving a wave, Ken hesitated, waiting for Philip to get into the car, but he didn't. He paused as if wanting to talk to Ken.

Realizing the man was trying to be friendly, Ken headed up the driveway. "Thanks again for inviting me to the barbecue last Sunday."

"Glad you could come." Philip gave him a warm smile, then looked down at his keys. "Nice to see you with Annie."

Ken only nodded, fighting the need to explain their relationship.

Philip pulled open the car door. "Jemma admires Annie and trusts her with Ellie. That's important to me."

"I can understand that," Ken said, puzzled about where Philip was going with the conversation.

"I think it's nice that you're dating."

Dating? Ken wanted to explain their friendship—how he'd helped her when her father fell and had happened to be there when her father needed EMS, but he stopped himself. He wasn't fooling anyone. Not Philip. Not himself. Annie had grown on him like whiskers. Though he shaved them off, they grew back…thicker, he often thought.

"Jemma thought you two might like to join us at

the ice cream social in a couple weeks. It's always fun.

Ken hesitated. "At the church?"

Philip chuckled. "No. I suppose churches are famous for them." He swung his hand toward town. "This is the 1223 Père Marquette Engine social. It's a tour of the old train. Kids can blow the whistle and ring the bell. They might even let a couple of us old guys give the bell a pull." A crooked grin etched his face. "Think about it. You can let us know."

Not waiting for Ken's response, Philip slid into his car, closed the door, and gave Ken a wave through the passenger window.

Ken stepped out of the way, letting him back down the driveway, then watched him until he vanished around the corner.

Heading toward the backyard, Ken's mind buzzed. Annie had stepped into his life and twisted it around. He'd lived with solitude for so long, but now, the taste of companionship eased over him with too much comfort. He liked having Annie to talk with. He loved the softness of her skin and the aroma of her flower-scented hair.

Remembering the feel of her lips on his woke the longing he had tried to forget. But Annie had not let him forget. Her smile, her tenderness, everything about her dragged his emotions out of their grave.

Now that Annie had gotten under his skin, he needed to be open with her or walk away. He'd said it before. Whatever he did, he didn't want to hurt Annie.

Hurt her? Their relationship had grown with each kiss. If he didn't have the guts to spill his story on the table, he had to go—hurt or no hurt.

But he wanted to find a way to break things off without making her feel responsible. Maybe moving again was the answer. He'd done that so often before. But this time he had his business. He hated to leave the only thing that had given him some pride and a sense of success.

He tilted his head back and closed his eyes. Could he tell Annie the truth? With foolish confidence, he'd told Cheryl, and she'd backhanded him with her reaction. The memory jolted him. Ken had to face it. He could no longer read people. No longer sense how they would react when they learned he had been a convict. Annie seemed so innocent, so pure, and he remembered her words that day when she'd said she feared he had some deep dire secret. How would she take the truth? He tossed around the possibilities like a hot potato. Tell her. Don't tell her.

He'd been a boy. A teenager. Years had passed since he'd been cornered in his buddy's cabin, shaking in his shoes. He had larger shoes now. Why did he make such a big deal out of it?

Because it had changed his life. But did it have to today? Gordon What's-his-name remembered Ken as a third-grader, not a man who'd served several years in prison.

He'd invested time and emotion in Annie's life. How could he walk away now…now when she was struggling with her future just as he was struggling with his own?

It all seemed to fit. He could keep his distance, steer Annie toward a job, maybe help her sell her paintings, then he could walk away before he hurt her. He could tell her he'd decided to move. She would understand and not take it personally.

He hated the idea, but it was all that he had—unless he plowed ahead and never told her the truth at all.

Annie stood beside her car in the Loving Care parking lot, surprised she'd decided to talk with Christie Hanuman. She'd been without a job for so long the idea of having one made her nervous. Besides nerves, the thought of getting up each morning, fighting the snow and ice in winter, missing her porch where she lolled in the summer, all of these thoughts aimed to push her back into her car. But reality kept her firm. She needed money to live and what better way to earn it than being with children? If she never had her own, she could enjoy someone else's.

Silence got to her, too. The silence in her life when Ken wasn't there. As strange as it seemed, she missed her father. Missed his demanding voice. Missed his frustrating commands. She'd gotten used to it in a strange way, the way people do when they have to…the way her mother had done. Tired of shedding useless tears over his passing, Annie needed to fill her time.

She eyed the neat ranch house, with its bright, decorated windows and the sign in front with its bright-blue lettering and the image of two clasped hands, one a child's, the other an adult's.

Garnering courage, Annie pushed the doorbell. She heard a pleasant *ding-dong* and waited. In a moment, a rather harried-looking woman opened the door. She eyed Annie as if looking for recognition. When she realized Annie didn't look familiar, she narrowed the gap in the door. "May I help you?"

"Christie Hanuman asked me to stop by to fill out a job application."

The woman's face brightened, and she widened the door opening. "Come in. Christie's in her office."

Annie stepped inside, admiring the bright pictures on the walls, the colorful bookshelves and two toy chests along with a small table surrounded by miniature chairs. The quiet in the house surprised her, and she glanced down the long hallway as the woman led her into the nearby kitchen.

In what had been a breakfast nook, Christie sat behind a small desk shuffling through a stack of papers. Hearing them enter, she lifted her head and looked at Annie with clear blue eyes. Recognizing her, her mouth curved in a smile.

"Annie. Right?"

Annie nodded. "We talked at Jemma's barbecue."

Christie stood and motioned to a chair near the desk. "Have a seat."

While Annie settled in the chair, Christie sat again and shifted the pile of work to the side, then folded her hands on her desk. "I'm so glad you decided to come."

Annie listened to the silence. "No children today?"

Christie laughed. "Nap time. One of those precious daily activities."

"I can imagine."

"When we're finished here, I'd be happy to show you around. It's almost time for naps to end so you'll get a better feel for our typical day."

"I'd love to have a look."

"So let's get down to business. My few full-time employees are vital. Most of them are part-time. I have a couple of high-school students right now, but they'll be going back to classes in another month or so. I need someone full-time who's dependable, prompt, rational—someone with common sense who won't panic with every problem."

Annie nodded, believing she was dependable, prompt and rational most of the time. Her thoughts went back to a few incidents with her father when she fell apart. She'd always been able to cope, but as time passed, she'd panicked more easily.

"Now the benefits," Christie said, handing her a sheet of paper.

Annie skimmed the list: the salary, group insurance, sick days, vacations. She weighed the responsibilities against the benefits.

Christie sat with her hands folded, watching Annie scan the list, her face set, without emotion.

Annie looked up and smiled. She liked Christie's business sense. She knew her job and knew what she wanted. Annie only wished she had the same confidence with her life.

"What do you think?" Christie asked.

"It looks good."

"Fine. I need to tell you that I have a couple more interviews scheduled. Two younger women with lots of experience, but I haven't spoken at length with either of them so I have no impressions."

Without warning, commotion echoed from the hallway.

"I understand," Annie said, sensing that her inexperience would be her downfall.

"Let me give you this application," Christine said, sliding a form across the desk. "Then we can look around."

Annie nodded, her confidence slipping a few notches when she thought about the younger women with more experience.

Christie rose and beckoned to her. "Let's take a look at the facility."

Annie followed, clutching her application as hope faded as quickly as her confidence.

# Chapter Eleven

Ken stood beside Annie's porch swing with the oil can. He tilted the narrow nozzle, giving the bottom a click-click, and watched the oil glaze the links. "Okay. Give it a try."

Annie sent him a grateful look and sat on the seat, then rocked back and forth, and for the first time, he heard nothing. No squeak. No creak.

"Silence," Annie said. "Thanks."

"I've been meaning to do that for an eternity." A couple months was all, but it seemed as if he'd been part of Annie's life forever.

Ken sank onto the wicker chair, though he would have preferred an invitation from Annie to sit beside her. He'd tried to keep his distance, but he'd failed. Tried to use common sense. Tried to maintain the friendship without letting his emotions get carried away like a lovesick teenager. At forty-five, he should have better control—but he didn't.

He ignored the yearning that jangled through him. "Have you heard anything from Loving Care?" he asked.

Annie shook her head while disappointment spread across her face. "I hate to call so soon. Christie mentioned she still had two other interviews, but she didn't mention when."

"How long has it been?"

"Two weeks. I dropped the application off the day after I went there." She rubbed the back of her neck and pulled at a few loose strands that had fallen from the knot of hair. "I figured it was hopeless, but you know me. I always have hope." As she spoke, Annie unsnapped the clasp and released her hair.

Ken couldn't speak, mesmerized by pale-gold strands like silken threads that tumbled onto her shoulders. The light shone through her hair, giving it an ethereal shimmer.

"What's wrong?" Annie asked.

"Nothing," he murmured, thinking everything seemed so right. "I've never seen your hair down before."

"I don't wear it that way," she said, rewinding the tendrils into a knot and catching it again with the clip.

"You should," he heard himself say.

She tilted her head. "Why?"

He had no answer except to say because she looked beautiful or because he wanted to run his fingers through it. "Just because," he said finally.

She grinned and curled her legs beneath her. "I've been thinking."

"Thinking?" His pulse galloped anticipating what she might say.

"I'm getting cold feet about showing my work to Claire."

Not what he'd expected, though he wasn't sure what he had thought she'd say. "Why?" The question sat uneasily on his thoughts. He'd hoped she would have done that sooner. He'd been disappointed, but Annie's life belonged to her not him. And he'd done so little with his own, how could he complain about what she did or didn't do?

Annie swung her feet to the floor. "I had high hopes about Loving Care. So far, nothing. Now I'm thinking the painting is my last option. What will I do if that falls through?"

He rose and slid beside her without an invitation. He caught her hand in his. "Don't look at it like that, Annie. You're the most hope-filled person I know. Where's your faith?"

"I have faith in God," she said, "but I don't always have faith in people."

Ken shut his mouth. That line of thinking he understood.

"I suppose I'm silly," Annie said.

Ken agreed. "Claire sounded positive. I'd give her a try."

"I suppose I should do that. I'll never know if I don't try."

"Good," he said. "Have you thought about the Père Marquette thing the Somervilles invited us to?" Where had that come from? He'd become his own worst enemy. His decisions were like putty. He plied them one way, then another depending if he were with Annie or away from her.

"It might be fun," she said.

"I talked with Philip again. He said we could meet at the Historical Museum in Grand Haven around seven."

Annie rose and straightened her knit top. "Sounds good." She stepped toward the door, then swung around to face him. "Come and help me."

"Help you?"

"I've just decided to choose which watercolors to show Claire."

His heart squeezed when her words sank in. He rose, and when he reached her, he wrapped his arms around her shoulders. *God, you call yourself faithful. Please don't let Annie down this time.*

Claire lifted a small painting from the carton and held it in the sunlight coming through the large storefront window. "I like this."

Trying to keep herself from being too hopeful, Annie clasped her hands in front of her and didn't speak.

Claire lifted another. "I like them all." Her look seemed matter-of-fact.

Annie's chest tightened, constricting her ability to breathe. She waited for Claire to continue.

Claire didn't.

Instead she placed the paintings back in the box that Annie had lugged into the store and pivoted, heading toward the counter.

With Claire's reaction, Annie released a ragged sigh, and her shoulders drooped. Listening to the woman's comments, she'd been so hopeful. It wasn't the money. What she wanted was purpose. That's what she needed more than income. Although if she were honest she needed that, too.

Her father's estate had been more than she expected, but she'd spent a few thousand of her inheritance on redecorating the living room, and she knew if she lived on the money too long it would dwindle away before she knew it.

Annie looked around the boutique, remembering the year she'd worked with Claire. "You don't happen to need any help in the shop, do you?" The words shot from her mouth before she could lasso them.

Claire spun around, her long denim skirt swishing above her colorful straw huaraches. "No. I already have my summer help. I'm so sorry, Annie. Had I known I'd—"

"No problem. The thought just crossed my mind." She wished the thought had stayed there. She was too old to grovel.

Claire drifted behind the counter and leaned down, locating something stored beneath. She rose and flipped through a booklet while Annie took a step backward, waiting for the moment to say goodbye.

Her discomfort heightened. She'd never begged for work in her life. For anything, for that matter, and now she wanted to escape. Obviously Claire had no interest in—

"Yes." Claire held up the booklet and pointed to

a page. "That will work." She beckoned Annie to look.

Pushing herself forward, Annie scanned the paper. A calendar, and beneath Claire's fingers she eyed the end of July.

"I don't understand," Annie said.

Claire's face brightened. "July 26 and 27 is Art in the Park. It's a juried show so you can add some prestige to your work."

Her meaning sank in. "You think I should put my work in an art show." Annie had hoped for a better idea than that. Not one day, but days when her water-colors would be shown in Claire's window.

"Don't you see my way of thinking?" Claire's face glowed with excitement. "You'll be able to call yourself a juried artist. It's perfect."

"But I wouldn't have time to—"

"I have connections. I know a person to talk with."

"I don't want special favors," Annie said.

Claire chuckled. "You think those judges would take something less than excellent to please me? You don't know anything about art connoisseurs."

"I suppose," Annie said, still doubting Claire's optimism.

"Then that's settled. You leave your work with me. I'll handle it."

Annie peered at the carton filled with her water-colors sitting near the window. Hoping her disappointment wasn't too evident, she forced a pleasant expression onto her face.

"After the art show when I put a sign in the window, juried artist, people will be impressed and your paintings will sell like hot cakes.''

Annie juggled her disjointed thoughts. ''You mean you still want to sell my work?''

''Did you have any doubt?''

Annie had had, but she didn't try to explain. She only smiled at Claire while her thoughts leaped to telling Ken.

Ken stepped out of the shower to the telephone's ring. He grabbed a towel, wrapped it around his waist and headed for the phone in his bedroom. He caught it on the fourth ring and gasped a hello.

''Ken?''

''Annie?'' Her voice surprised him. He knew calling was difficult since she still held on to the outdated male-dominant idea.

''You're out of breath,'' Annie said.

''I was in the shower.'' Her voice had an unfamiliar ring. ''Is something wrong?''

''Not really.''

*Not really.* That meant something had happened. ''So, what's up?''

''I remembered you suggested we visit the nursery so I could check out some shrubs and new garden flowers for the landscaping. Is tonight good for you?''

He grinned as her invitation shot down his old-fashioned concept of her. Still, something was up. He sensed it. ''Sure, it's good for me.''

''Great. What time?'' she asked.

''How about six-thirty?''

"I'll see you in a bit, then."

He said goodbye and put down the receiver, his mind conjuring up the real reason why Annie had called. Something important. It had to be. He dried off and pulled clothes from the closet, finding himself hurrying as if he had something urgent needing his immediate attention.

When he'd finished, Ken glanced at his wristwatch. Six o'clock. He pondered his decision. Wait or go early?

Curiosity won out. He couldn't wait.

He locked the door, and once on the road, his mind wandered. First his concern headed for Annie's unusual call, but his next thought drifted to his mother's New Testament.

Annie had set it on the table weeks earlier, and he'd left it there without touching it—only staring at it as if it were a wild animal he needed to keep his eye on.

But words he'd heard recently kept drifting into his thoughts. *God is faithful. God hears prayer. Jesus is the way.* Sometimes he wanted to push the phrases away. Life seemed easier when he didn't have to deal with those religious sentiments. But Annie's sure faith softened his thinking.

He pictured a few evenings earlier, sitting alone in the living room, when Annie's words had come to him. *The end of that verse is my favorite,* "And now these three remain: faith, hope and love. But the greatest of these is love."

Surprising himself, Ken had picked up the small

testament and thumbed through the pages. He remembered the verse had come from First something. The letter *C* came to mind. Leaves flashed passed as he thumbed until he caught a name. That was it. First Colossians. He grinned when he saw his error, but the next time through, he found what he had been looking for. First Corinthians.

He scanned the pages until he'd spotted the words. Pausing, he read them again, but this time he continued on. In chapter sixteen, he read, then reread the message. *Be on your guard; stand firm in the faith; be men of courage; be strong. Do everything in love.*

Faith? Courage? Strong? How long had it been since he felt like a man of courage? He needed courage to tell Annie about his past. Courage to be free of the fears he'd lived with so long. Courage to admit he was falling in love. *Do everything in love.*

The words knotted in his stomach. He wasn't falling in love.

He'd already fallen.


Annie stood at the sink with a vase, arranging a few flowers from the garden. She loved a fresh bouquet. Though urging Ken to the nursery had been a ploy to get to tell him about Claire's decision, Annie was eager to see the new flowers and other changes in her landscaping.

*Changes.* Her house. Now her garden. Was that the kind of change she really longed for—or could it be she wanted to change herself? Her life?

She let the uneasy thought slip from her mind and

envisioned the evening. She'd try to hold off the surprise as long as she could just to tease him. She suspected he knew something was up.

Ken had been so eager for her to do something with her paintings. He'd given her support and encouragement from the beginning. He'd been someone who stood by her side as no one else had—except perhaps her brother Bill. He'd been a true friend.

*Friend.* The word skittered across her chest. She'd dreamed of something more. Ken's few kisses and gentle touches had caused her to look at the relationship in a different light, but he'd made no move to suggest it was anything more than friendship. She would have to cherish that.

Glancing at her watch, Annie looked out the window like a girl waiting for her first date. He wasn't due for another half hour, but she was anxious to get the evening rolling. She'd never thought how important her artwork could be. Tonight she felt alive, the way she did in Ken's arms.

She left the window, looked in the mirror to check her makeup. After looking outside again, she pushed open the front door. Though the evening air still radiated heat, it had become cooler. Annie stepped onto the porch.

"Yoo-hoo. How are you today, dear?" Abby's voice sailed across the distance.

"Okay." She walked to the side of the porch to speak to the woman who'd been so kind…always.

"If you ever want company, dear, you just let us know. Sissy and I would enjoy having you visit."

Annie smiled. ''Thank you. I'll do that.'' She held her breath, wondering what Abby really wanted.

''We'd love to come over to see your new furniture.''

Annie cringed, realizing she'd been neglectful. ''Yes. How about tomorrow?''

''That would be fine, dear,'' Abby said, giving her a wave and heading back into the house, Annie was certain, to tell Sissy they'd been invited.

She turned back toward the door, and eyeing the swing, she smiled, picturing Ken clicking the oil can to quiet the creaky chains. She eased her back against the cushion, wondering what life would be like if she and Ken were married. She pictured them sitting on the porch swing, an old married couple reminiscing about the past and how they'd met.

Tires crunched on the driveway, and Annie straightened her back and stretched her neck to see over the porch wall. Ken. Already. She glanced at her watch, then stood to greet him.

After he'd exited the car, he gave her a sheepish wave and headed up the porch steps. ''I'm early.''

''You are,'' she said. ''But that's no problem. We'll have more daylight at the nursery.''

He bounded up the porch stairs, and they stood face to face. The scent of soap and earthy aftershave clung to his skin, like a walk in the woods on a summer's day—pine, cedar and a hint of musk. Annie longed to run her fingers through his hair or touch the smoothness of his clean-shaven cheek.

''Ready?'' she asked. ''I'll run and get my purse.''

"I'll wait out here," he said, motioning to a chair.

Annie hurried inside and returned with her handbag.

Ken rose, and she followed him to the car, struggling to hold back her good news until later. During the ride, Annie talked about everything under the sun while Ken listened with an occasional comment.

The nursery's sign appeared on the right, and Ken pulled into the parking lot.

"Let's look outside first," he suggested, "while we have the light."

She agreed and followed him past the building along the path discussing the virtues of barberry versus arborvitae, rose of Sharon versus spirea until Annie spotted a gazebo and arched trellises forming cozy arbors with benches. She headed for one large swing canopied by a trellis with climbing roses. With no customers nearby, the quiet setting drew her forward.

"How about this?" she asked, giving Ken a bright smile. "More chains to oil."

He shook his head and followed her as she slid onto the cozy wooden swing.

Ken sat beside her, his palm resting against her hand, as the swing swayed in slow rhythm. Tonight his touch seemed different. Heat penetrated her skin and she sensed a tender intimacy—a familiar acceptance—in his action.

He shifted closer, and his husky voice broke the stillness. "You have something to tell me."

"Is that a question?" she asked, knowing it wasn't.

"A statement."

"What makes you think that?"

His soft chuckle mixed with his words. "You rarely call me...except on business."

She shrugged. "This was business. Anyway, can't a woman change?"

"Something happened," he said, ignoring her question.

"I saw Claire, that's all."

He pivoted and looked into her eyes. "You did?"

Loving his excitement, Annie related the details of her visit with Claire.

Ken's face brightened. "Annie. That's such good news." His eyes searched hers, reflecting a personal joy at hearing the story. He ran his finger along her cheek and captured her chin in his palm before his lips met hers.

The tender kiss deepened, and Annie's heart surged with emotion, enjoying the strength of his mouth against hers, his firm lips, the feel of sinew flexing beneath her hands, sensing how good and right it all seemed.

Ken eased back, his eyes glazed with emotion, but beneath his weighted lids, she sensed his own surprise.

Annie caught her breath. "Do you like it?"

"The kiss or the swing?"

"Both," she said, pleased that he hadn't apologized for kissing her. Filled with hope, she bounded from the swing and twirled to face him.

The swing jarred backward, then rocked forward as Ken secured his feet to the ground and grasped the seat arm to steady himself. Steady his thoughts…and his pulse.

Ken looked at her smiling eyes, glinting in the summer sun. The kiss lingered on his lips, the sweetness of her mouth, her small gasping breaths, her heart beating next to his. He loved it. Could he answer her differently. "Forget the swing, but I loved the kiss."

She held out her hand, and he grasped it and rose. Friendship is what he'd planned, but the kiss…that kiss had deepened their relationship even more. Now he had to think. Throw his fears in the air and let himself love her.

The warmth of her hand against his surged through him. He cherished her. He had no doubt. But if he stayed, did he have enough courage to tell her about his past? And could she forgive him? Maybe as time passed…

Ken stopped his dreaming. Annie deserved a good man, and a good Christian man. He wasn't either— at least not one with the kind of faith that Annie had.

Annie looked up at him, her smile warm and loving.

He'd let fate decide. Fate. God. Weren't they one in the same? The words flew back and smacked him in the chest. *Be on your guard; stand firm in the faith; be men of courage; be strong. Do everything in love.*

That's what he'd do. Do everything in love. If the God Annie professed wanted to bless a sinner, Ken offered the Lord a chance to work a miracle on him.

# *Chapter Twelve*

Expecting the Hartmann sisters any minute, Annie kept her ear tuned for the doorbell. She heard their footsteps and chatter before they pushed the button, and she surprised them by opening the door.

"You heard us," Abby said, stepping back and beckoning Sissy to go ahead of her into the house.

"I was watching for you," Annie said, closing the door behind them.

She watched their eyes widen as they moved from the foyer into the living room.

"So pretty," Sissy said. "Don't you think so, Abby?"

"Very nice," she agreed, standing in the middle of the room, her hands folded in front of her. "The upholstery is cheerier, and the sun comes through the windows."

"You have new curtains," Sissy said.

Annie brushed the lighter lace fabric. "Yes. The

curtains and some new furniture. I wanted to get new carpet but decided not to get carried away.''

The sisters chuckled, then stood waiting.

''Would you like to sit in here? I hope coffee's all right.''

''That's fine, dear,'' Abby said.

''Let's sit here and enjoy the room,'' Sissy said.

While they selected seats, Annie headed for the kitchen, happy to get the ''duty'' visit over with. She couldn't help but be fond of the sisters. They'd been part of her life forever it seemed, but sometimes their visits were tedious and too filled with town news, as they called it. Annie called it gossip.

When they were busy with guests at Loving Arms, she almost missed hearing their ''yoo-hoo'' from across the lawn.

Aware of their conversation from the living room, Annie hurried to fill a carafe and carried it into the living room. Abby and Sissy had chosen the sofa, so Annie set the tray on the coffee table in front of them. She poured the brew into cups and let them add their own fixings.

''Are you busy next door?'' Annie asked to break the silence.

''Yes indeed,'' Abby said. ''Poor Mr. Stillwell is with us. His sister, Rudy, do you remember her? She's in the nursing home here in town and very ill.''

''That's too bad,'' Annie said. ''I think I know her from Fellowship Church.''

''And our niece is coming to visit on Friday,'' Sissy said. ''She has a booth at Art in the Park just like you do. We were so surprised to hear from her. Naturally we won't charge her for the room."

Annie swallowed a laugh. "That's nice. I'm sure you'll enjoy her visit. Does she paint, too?" Annie took a sip from her cup.

"No. She makes jewelry. So Sissy and I will be going to the park art show."

Annie took a sip from her cup. "Don't forget to drop by my booth."

"Oh, we will," Sissy said.

"Does your niece live far?" Annie asked.

"In Cadillac. She's about your age, I think." Sissy looked at Abby for assurance.

"Nancy's a little older, I'd say."

Cadillac. The city name pinged in Annie's mind. "What a coincidence. Ken Dewitt grew up in Cadillac."

"He did?" Abby said, her eyebrows lifting. "Perhaps he knows Nancy."

"He might," Annie said, sorry she'd mentioned it. Annie recalled Ken's discomfort talking to people from his past—people like Gordon Henley. She hoped the woman didn't know him.

The conversation tightened in her chest like a noose.

Annie stood back and watched Ken inside the canvas enclosure while he hammered and nailed wood, hinges and pegboard, creating a portable backdrop to display her watercolors for the Art in the Park. All around them, green-and-white striped tents dotted the expanse of grass—booths filled with oils and water-colors, sculptures, pottery and jewelry of all kinds.

"I think that'll do it," Ken said, stepping from beneath the canopy to view his handiwork. He studied the structure for a moment, then gave Annie a grin and wandered to her side. "Well?" He slid his arm around her waist.

"Perfect," she said, enjoying the closeness and the warmth of his hand against her side. His skin smelled of sunshine and cedar. "Now all we need to do is set it up."

"Let's get to work," he said, giving her waist a squeeze. He shifted his arm and headed for the boxes they'd set inside the tent.

Annie watched him a moment, admiring his strong features, his determined mouth and the dimple beneath that deepened as he set his mind to the task. Ken had gotten a haircut, and Annie noticed the whiter coloring around his hairline where the sun had been unable to penetrate.

When he bent down to lift her paintings from the crate, Annie joined him inside the booth. In the shadow of the enclosure, she paused a moment to brush her fingers along the nape of his neck. "Nice haircut," she said, feeling giddy with the awakening of her feelings.

"Thanks." He captured her fingers and drew them to his lips.

"I should be thanking you," Annie said. "I couldn't have done this without you."

"I wanted to help."

"I know. I just hope—"

"Stop worrying. You'll sell your work."

"You think so?"

He nodded.

Feeling more hopeful than she had in weeks, Annie worked along with Ken as he attached the watercolors to the board, selecting ones that complemented each other, arranging smaller paintings with larger ones to give the display balance.

When he'd hung the last frame, Annie arranged the two large paintings on easels she'd brought along, tilting them to best catch the sun.

The canvas flapped and fluttered, and concerned, Annie paused before moving to the tent's opening to look at the sky. Clouds had come from nowhere. Within minutes, the bright sky had turned a misty gray. "Looks like rain."

Ken stepped from beneath the canvas. "Maybe it'll hold off."

Looking at the small tent, then the expanse of grass where people would meander to view each artist's work, Annie's optimism darkened. She wondered how many buyers would venture out on a rainy day. Disillusioned, she studied the wind as it rustled the trees, sending their branches dipping and swaying. The canvas sides snapped as they flapped in and out with the wind's pressure.

Ken moved to the back of the booth and gathered his tools. With no one apt to show up if it rained, Annie stood in the opening alone, concentrating on thinking positively—and on smiling—just in case people did come.

When she really thought about it, selling her paintings had been Ken's idea, not hers. He'd been the one who wanted her life to have meaning. Although she had to agree, she needed to do something after her father died.

Her father's death had settled over like one of the storm clouds, leaving her as jumpy as a jack-in-the-box. She never knew when tears would pop into her eyes. Never knew when she'd feel a rush of emptiness or a twinge of regret.

Life had never been easy with her father. Her mother had been a gracious, Christian woman who worked hard to see a positive side even in the worst situation. When her father came staggering home late from work and went to bed too drunk to eat, Annie's mother would tell the children how nice it was to have a quiet evening alone with just them. When the money had gone to liquor and not food, her mother had taught the children how to make the most of little…and always with love. Sometimes Annie wondered how her mother could love her father at all during the bad times.

"Why so quiet?" Ken asked, moving beside her with an armload of leftover wood and his toolbox.

"Just thinking."

He didn't say anything, and Annie wondered if Ken realized how quiet he was most of the time. She'd known him for a year, and though they'd become closer, she still knew so little. Like a puzzle, she gathered one piece at a time, but the pieces were rare and didn't always fit.

"Thinking? About what?" he asked as if her words had finally sunk in.

To answer, she shifted her thoughts. "About Pa. Sometimes I wonder how my mother endured all those years with his problems—drinking and wasting money. We lived in fear and embarrassment. Mom's faith, I suppose, and marriage vows—for better or worse."

Ken winced. Annie's attitude jarred his memory. He'd been a drinker, created fear, embarrassed his family, and caused them shame. *For better or worse.* Annie's words crept like tendrils through his conscience. His life had been worse not better. Since running into Gordon, the old days kept niggling at him and brought back fear of discovery. He wished the guy hadn't remembered him.

Annie's words rang in his head, but before he needed to say anything, thunder tumbled through the sky like unleashed oil drums. A bolt of lightning zigzagged across the heavens, ripping a hole in the heavy clouds and sending a torrent pouring down in thick sheets.

Ken jumped back and dropped his armload while the wind charged forward in savage gusts snagging up a front tent peg from the ground. The side canvas drooped and flapped wildly in the downpour.

Annie yelled and jerked her easel away from the opening. Ken caught it before the painting fell to the ground. He handed her the frame, then charged forward and gripped the guy rope. After pulling it firmly into place, he bent down to retrieve the peg.

"Hand me a hammer," he called to Annie, the rain washing over him like Niagara Falls.

Squinting against the downpour, he watched Annie fumble in his toolkit. When she found the hammer, she hurried to him. Once the hammer met his hand, she darted back out of the rain.

With slippery fingers and eyes blinded by the water, Ken tightened the guy rope, then hammered the peg deep into the ground. He gave it a tug and, confident it was secure, he stepped back inside the tent.

"You're sopped," Annie said, hovering beside him. "I'm sorry."

"Not your fault." A chill ran up his back as he wiped his face with the bottom of his dripping shirt and sank into the corner chair. He wished he could escape, but until the wind died down, he wanted to be there to keep an eye on the tent pegs.

Annie stood beside him, staring at the rain, and his thoughts drifted back to their conversation. Only days earlier, Ken had decided to push the past aside and face the present, perhaps even look to the future. Time had passed. He had changed, and over the years, his life had slogged along straight and honest. He'd built his own business, earning enough money to live well. And now he'd met Annie.

Since facing his feelings, Ken had given up fighting his emotions. He longed to give their relationship a try. To let it grow. Yet today, Annie's comment settled uneasily in his mind. Would her life with him be for better or worse? He hoped for better.

"Speaking of quiet," Annie said, "you're no bundle of conversation. You must feel miserable." She moved a chair and sat beside him.

"I'm okay," he said, while his sodden clothes sent a chill through his body. "A little rain never hurt anybody."

She looked through the tent opening to the cloud-laden sky. "Rain. Why today?" She shook her head. "It's depressing."

"It'll pass."

"I can't believe you're sitting there soaking wet and being so optimistic."

While the sky rumbled and flashed, silence settled over them. Annie folded her arms across her chest, looking forlorn and discouraged. Finally she rubbed the back of her neck and shifted closer to Ken.

Her unsettling gaze caught his. "Why do you always hide in corners?"

"I'm not hiding. I'm waiting for the rain to stop."

"It's not just today. You're nervous whenever we get around people."

Her comment charged along his spine. Why had she decided to push him now, during the storm when he felt trapped? "I'm not a people person. You know that."

"You are with me." She leaned closer, searching his eyes. "You are with Philip…and with Claire. It's strangers, Ken. It's as if you're afraid of something, or someone. I wish you'd tell me about it. Let me know what's eating at you.''

Ken had heard that before. Cheryl had asked the same questions. ''Tell me. I'll understand.'' But people didn't understand. Christians didn't understand. He caught himself, realizing the comment wasn't fair. Not all Christians, but many.

''It's nothing, Annie.''

''It's nothing you want to tell me, you mean.''

Disappointment filled her face, and Ken wanted to disappear. To run as he'd always done. But now things were different. Annie had given him a spark of hope, a faint light. Her faith. Her God. If only he could believe fully. If only he could really let it all go and give it to the Lord as Annie kept telling him.

''I had a bad family life, Annie. I told you enough.'' He gestured toward the tent's opening. ''Look, the rain's letting up. People will be coming.''

Annie glanced outside, then refocused to him. ''I owe you a lot, Ken. You've become important to me. You can't keep shutting me out. Either we're friends or...''

She stopped, and a sigh lifted her shoulders. Ken wanted to take her in his arms, to hold her to tell her the awful details. All of it, but fear rose up like bile and he couldn't.

''We're good friends, Annie.'' He reached over and grasped her hand. ''Another day I'll tell you what I can.''

''About Gordon Henley?''

He shook his head. ''I honestly don't remember

him, but I'll tell you what I remember. I've blocked out so much of my youth.''

With her face etched with sadness, Annie lifted his hand and kissed his fingers. ''I don't mean to pry, Ken. I care and I just want to…''

Hearing voices, Ken shifted his gaze to the opening in time to see a couple from Fellowship Church holding a large umbrella stop in front of the booth. Annie rose and hurried to greet them.

He sat again, not wanting to make small talk, only wanting to escape before someone else showed up who might remember Ken Dewitt from Cadillac. Instead, he listened to the slowing pat-patter of raindrops hitting the canvas roof.

The couple wandered into the tent, gave him a nod, and ambled through the display looking at one picture after another. Ken felt out of place, and the thoughts that Annie had dredged up drifted back to his life in Cadillac—things he'd longed to forget but never would.

He tuned back to the present, just in time to witness Annie's first sale. A small painting, but a sale. She handed him the cash, and while she wrapped the painting in tissue and brown paper, he made change from the cash box she'd brought along. He felt as much pride as if the watercolor were his own.

When the couple said goodbye, Annie spun around, her smile genuine, as if their talk had never occurred. ''Can you believe it?''

''I can. I told you.'' He took her in his arms and

held her close, enjoying the moment and wishing the good feeling could last forever.

She drew in a lengthy breath as if she felt the same.

Hearing sounds, she turned to the front of the booth to greet another brave couple as they passed. Ken admired her for that. Annie had a natural way with people. Even after those years of living for her parents, she hadn't lost her innate love for individuals, and it showed on her face.

For a moment the sun peeked from behind a cloud and shone through the summer sprinkle. Annie seemed to light up. The rays glimmered through her light-colored hair, causing her to glow. Ken liked the outfit she'd worn today. Comfortable shoes, for one. Annie was never afraid to wear something less glamorous for the sake of comfort. She wore a coral top, and her long colorful skirt brushed her ankles. Even in the rain, Annie looked like sunshine.

Another couple stopped, and as they talked, Ken heard the raindrops overhead slow and, finally, fade away. When the couple had gone, Annie stood alone a moment before moving closer to Ken.

"The rain's stopped," Annie said. "I hope that ends it."

He rose and patted the chair. "Sit while you have a chance. You have a long day."

She didn't move, and Ken slipped his arm around her shoulder and drew her nearer. "I think I'll get out of here while I have the chance." He shifted away and reached down to gather up the wood and toolbox.

"You're leaving?"

He straightened the wood under his arm. "I'm in the way here. And besides, I'm wet."

"You're not in the way, but you are wet."

"I'll be back later to help you pack up."

She followed him to the opening, her flowery scent wrapping around him while he struggled to keep his thoughts as cheery as her fragrance.

He gave her a wave and kept going. He didn't have the heart to look back.

For better or worse? He had no idea.

# *Chapter Thirteen*

Annie held the door while Ken carried in the last carton of paintings. "Thanks so much. You've been a lifesaver."

"You want this in the same place?"

"Might as well," Annie said, leading the way into the dining room. "I have to get some of these over to Claire so I can see what she wants."

Ken plopped the box beside the other. "At least you came back with less than you took over there."

Annie brushed some stray hairs from her face. She felt tired, yet excited about the long day. "I did fairly well despite the rainstorm."

"I told you so," Ken said, brushing her cheek with his finger. "I piled the display stand and easels along the wall of the garage."

"Thanks."

Annie beckoned him to the living room. She

plopped into a chair and leaned her head back for a moment. "I'm exhausted. Too much smiling."

Ken stood in the doorway and chuckled. "Mind if I get us something to drink?"

Annie bolted upright. "I'm sorry. I should have offered—"

"Don't be silly. I've been around here enough to ask when I want something. And I did."

"Bring me some iced tea, if you would," she called, returning her head to the chair back and closing her eyes.

Hearing Ken opening cabinets in the kitchen gave her a comfortable feeling. The way it should be with a man and a woman who'd spent so much time together. She smiled, feeling cozy and contented.

"Here you go," Ken said, holding out the glass.

Annie opened her eyes and took the tumbler from him.

He sank into the sofa and took a long drink of cola.

Annie slipped off her shoes, then curled her feet beneath her. "Did I tell you who came to my booth?"

"You mentioned Jemma and Ellie."

"Jemma bought a little seascape. She said she had a small sailboat painting that would look nice as a grouping." She sipped the tea. "The Hartmanns dropped by. Their niece had a booth with handcrafted jewelry. She's from Cadillac."

Ken's head shot upward, but he didn't respond.

"Her name is Nancy something. Nancy Barnes, or maybe it was Burns." Annie watched his expression darken. She knew she should shut her mouth, but cu riosity drove her forward.

Ken only shrugged.

Annie reined in the questions that were ready to leap from her mouth. He'd promised to tell her later and she'd have to have patience. One thing she'd learned about Ken. She couldn't push him. He had to make his own decisions about when to talk—in his time, not hers. She chuckled to herself. Sort of like the Lord. She couldn't rush Him either.

They settled into an easy silence. Ken shifted on the sofa, leaning against the corner and stretching his legs along the cushion, his shoes extending over the edge. He appeared relaxed and at home in her house. The image warmed her like a fleece blanket.

Thinking of Ken's family had caused Annie's recollections to drift to her own. She raised her head from the chair back. "Something I said earlier today struck me. Something that made me think."

Ken took a sip of cola, his eyes focused on her.

"About my father," she said. "And my mother's faithfulness to him. I sounded so ungrateful and unloving." She slid her feet from beneath her and rested them on the floor.

"Ungrateful?"

"My dad had problems. I've told you the stories. He drank and wasted money, he missed birthday parties and ruined holidays, but he stuck around and he didn't beat us. He just had problems."

Ken's face flickered with misgiving. "That's a bonus."

The coldness of his words cut through her. "I realize you don't look at things like I do." Neither did her siblings, and seeing the look on Ken's face disappointed her. "But I believe in the commandments, and I honored my parents the best I could. My mother was easy. She was a saint." A ragged breath shivered from her chest, being reminded of losing her father.

"And you've forgiven your sisters, too. And what about the brother who didn't show up to the funeral?" He lowered his feet and straightened.

"Roy. Yes, I forgive them all. I don't forget, Ken. I can't forget how they behave, but I can't spend my life angry and frustrated. Life is too short. Forgiveness doesn't mean you like what happened. It doesn't mean you want it to happen again. It means you show them grace. Mercy. That's what God does. He doesn't like what we do, but we're his children. He loves us. He forgives us."

Annie studied his face to see if he understood. "I guess what I'm trying to say is I forgave Pa for his wrongdoings because he had a flaw. Problems he didn't understand and didn't know how to control."

"You call that a *flaw?*" His brows knitted above his darkened eyes.

"Alcoholism. Yes, it's a disease. A flaw that a person can't control alone, and he ended up paying for it. His carousing took a toll on his health. I never want to end up the last years of my life in a hospital bed being cared for by my chil…by anyone."

The statement stabbed her heart. She'd never have the children to care for her even if she needed it.

"So you forgave him."

"I did, and believe it or not, I miss him even though he was often like a sliver in my finger. Constant irritation and sometimes pain. Still, I loved him because he was my father."

Ken patted the sofa beside him and beckoned her, his eyes reflecting his understanding.

Annie rose and crossed the carpet. "And do you realize—" she said sitting beside him "—I even received a reward. My father left me this house and part of the annuity we didn't even know he had. God works things out. We just have to let Him have free rein."

As she finished the sentence, the telephone rang.

Ken turned his gaze toward the cordless phone on the table, but she decided to catch the call in the kitchen. She rose and headed through the doorway.

Everything Annie had said since they'd arrived home settled on Ken's mind. Nancy Burns. The name had struck him. Jack Burns. One of the friends who'd escaped the break-in punishment had dated a girl named Nancy. Jack's aunt had owned the cottage they'd vandalized. Could Jack have married Nancy? When he heard her name, it had charged through him like electricity.

Annie's voice lilted through the doorway. The call was pleasant, he could tell from her tone.

Annie. A woman who always looked for the positive in a negative. She amazed him. *Forgiveness.* She'd said the word so simply. Not like a victim. Only the simple statement. *I forgave him.*

He rubbed his head, trying to imagine the freedom found in forgiveness. Like a weight being lifted from his back. Like shackles dropping from his wrists and ankles. He'd spent his childhood being told that God punished. He'd spent his life hiding from his past. Annie had forgiven hers. The idea overwhelmed him.

When he heard the conversation end in the kitchen, Ken rose, and Annie came through the doorway.

"She wants me," she said, her voice bubbling with happiness.

"Who?"

"Christie Hanuman. I have the job." She clasped her hands against her chest. "I can't believe it."

"At the child care?"

She nodded and joyful tears glistened in her eyes. "I start this Monday. Can you believe?"

"Why not? You always amaze me."

She shook her head. "I'm excited and...nervous."

Annie's face glowed with joy, and her eyes glinted with tears and happiness. Ken opened his arms and took her into his embrace.

She buried her face against his shoulder and laughed against his chest. The feeling filled him with unbelievable contentment. The way life should be. Sharing, caring, laughing, crying, loving. He'd never known a relationship like this one. Not even with Cheryl.

"I'm happy for you," he whispered into her hair.

She tilted her face to his. "I know you are. You wanted me to get a life, and now I have one, one that's overflowing. Selling my watercolors and a job with kids. I feel like a teenager looking forward to my first day's work.''

''And don't forget Claire's offer.''

''I know. It's amazing.'' She tilted her face upward, her eyes shining.

You're amazing, he thought. Her tender look reflected all that he desired—a loving wife, a family.

He lowered his mouth to brush a kiss against her perfect lips, his chest tightening with emotion. He eased back, taking in her gentle face. He was forty-five. She, a little younger. Annie could still be a mother. He could be a father. A good father. One who showed his love and supported his child's dreams. He'd never had love or support, and he knew Annie could give him both. Did he want to be a free man or a prisoner in his own self-contained world? Yet, he felt so unworthy of a woman like Annie.

He needed to think. To plan his course. To decide once and for all.

Would he live life or let it die?

Annie stood at the doorway, greeting parents and saying goodbye to the children. Her work at Loving Care had proven a blessing, filling her time and distracting her from Ken.

She knew he struggled with something, and she couldn't stop pushing. Why didn't he understand that if he laid his cares on the Lord he'd be free?

For a while she'd feared Ken wanted to move on. To leave her behind. She wondered if it were her beliefs. But recently, she'd been encouraged by the changes she'd seen in him. He'd begun to ask questions about God and faith.

Maybe she had hope. Just maybe, if she could be patient—which seemed to be her eternal problem.

Better to lay off. Annie wished she had earlier, but she had probed. She wanted answers, and controlling that flaw in her character had always been difficult.

For years she'd keep things about herself private. She'd tried not to complain or whine about her life. She'd plastered a smile on her face and gone to church or chatted with the Hartmann sisters. Other than the kind ladies from Fellowship Church, people like Jemma, she had never known a close girlfriend, at least not since high school.

Feeling the tug on her skirt, Annie looked down at a small upturned face. "Good-bye, Mandy." The child spread open her arms, and Annie knelt down to give the child a bear hug.

The girl's mother grinned. "She thinks you're tops."

"I think she's tops," Annie said, uncurling her tired legs and longing for the day to end.

Mandy waved as her mother grabbed her other hand to guide her through the doorway.

Work at the child-care center not only filled Annie's time, she felt loved and needed. Her longing to be a mother could be fulfilled, in part, by spending time with the little ones.

"Good job," Christie said, coming to Annie's side. "I made the right choice. You're really great with kids and I have great confidence in you."

"Thanks. I like it here a lot."

"Are you divorced or widowed?" Christie asked.

Annie shook her head. "Neither. I've never married." She stopped herself from relaying the long story of caring for her sick father. She'd told it enough, and now she had moved on. No need to wallow in the old self-sacrifice.

"Too bad," Christie said. "You'd be a great mother."

Annie shrugged. "Maybe, but it's too late now."

"Never too late. Agencies are dying for women like you to foster children." She rested her hand on Annie's arm. "And you're still young enough to be a mother yourself."

A sputtered laugh flew from Annie's throat. "Not without a husband. At least not this lady."

"You have a point there, but I'm sure you have a few single men beating at your door."

Though she sent Annie a sweet smile, Annie didn't respond to the comment. She had one man who wasn't beating exactly, but who meant more to her than she could say.

"What about you?" Annie asked, noticing Christie didn't wear a wedding band. "Are you married?"

This time Christie laughed. "Did that once. Never again."

Annie opened her mouth to ask why, but remembering the woman was her boss and she a new employee, she stopped her question. Still, curiosity rumbled through her. What had happened in Christie's life? Death? Divorce?

One final child stood near the door, and in seconds, a mother came through filled with apologies for being late. She hugged her son and with a final goodbye, Annie breathed a relieved sigh and gathered her belongings.

"Busy evening?" Christie asked.

Annie grinned. "It's not a hot date, if that's what you're thinking. I have an appointment to meet with Claire Dupre. She owns Loving Treasures on Washington."

"Appointment?"

"She's agreed to show my artwork in her shop. My watercolors."

Christie's face brightened. "Really? That's great. I didn't know you painted."

"I did. For years. Just for my own amusement. Something to do on those long, lonely nights." She felt the need to explain. "I spent years caring for ailing parents."

"That's a difficult situation," Christie said. "And so common now."

Annie shrugged. "It's what the Lord asks us to do."

"You're a Christian, then."

Christie's comment had no undertone—no judgement one way or the other, but the way she said it puzzled Annie. She studied Christie's face, looking for an indicator. Finally she asked, "You're not a believer?"

Christie shrugged. "I wouldn't say that. I believe in a higher power. God, if you will. I just like depending on me. I have more control. I'm my own boss.''

Her words bounced inside Annie's mind. What could she say to make a difference? *Father, give me words.* "That's what I love about the Lord. He's created us in His image. He's given us free will to choose. In that sense, we are our own bosses.''

"You think so?" Christie said.

Annie could see she was struggling with the concept. "I'm confident in that. I've made lots of mistakes in my life. Too many to admit. If the Lord had total control, I wouldn't make mistakes. Bad things wouldn't happen. This would be heaven.''

"It's not heaven. You can say that again.''

Annie forced herself to chuckle and decided to back off. She'd given Christie something to think about. She'd made the same mistake with Ken. People needed to find the Lord in their own time. She couldn't rush the process.

Annie took a step backward toward the door. "Well, I'd better get.''

"Good night, Annie. See you tomorrow.''

Annie gave her a wave and hurried outside.

She slipped into her car and drove toward Loving Treasures. Her mind wrestled with thoughts of Ken and of Christie until they drifted to her appointment with Claire. Though the air-conditioning hummed full blast, her hand became clammy wondering what would happen today. Claire had said she would display her work on consignment. But what did she mean? One painting? Two? Or a box full?

What difference did it make? If she sold one, Claire would take another, then another. And if she sold everything, she'd keep painting. Ken had encouraged her recently to set up her easel. He'd been her inspiration in so many ways.

Thinking of the past, Annie realized how she'd allowed the situation to box her into a corner. She'd hidden behind her parents' illnesses rather than make a life of her own. She hadn't realized it until now—until Ken had encouraged her to open the door and step outside. Hiding had been too easy. Poor Annie. Martyr to her family. The words wrenched through her. Could it be she liked the role?

The Loving Treasures sign appeared ahead of her, and Annie pulled in the side parking lot and carried her smallest box to the side door of the shop. She balanced the carton low on one knee and rang the bell.

In moments, Claire appeared with a smile and pushed open the door. "Hi. I've been waiting for you."

"Sorry," Annie said, "I got out of work a little late."

"No problem. I'm just anxious."

Claire grasped the box from Annie's hand and set it on a worktable inside the back room. "Is this all you brought?"

"No. I have more in the car."

"Bring them in," she said, her attention already turned to removing Annie's artwork from the carton. Feeling less concern, Annie hurried to the car and opened the trunk. She eyed the two larger paintings and decided to let those stay. Instead, she hoisted the other container and slammed the trunk.

Wriggling with the box on her hip, she opened the back door and made her way inside.

"I love this," Claire called from the workroom.

Annie came through the doorway as Claire held up a still life she'd painted. An oriental fan beside a red vase filled with Fuji mums.

"Thank you," Annie said, realizing the bright colors and exotic flavor of the painting matched Claire's typical garb. Today she had toned her appearance down to a crinkle gauze skirt in teal with a matching big-size shirt. Colorful beads wound beneath the collar and a matching clip caught her wild red hair to one side.

"Here's my thought," Claire said, lining the smaller frames along the work table. "I can display the smaller ones on a stand near the window and hang the larger ones behind the counter." She stepped back and gestured to the wall. "What do you think? Enough light there?"

"I would think so," Annie said, amazed at Claire's enthusiasm.

"You know, we have a problem," Claire said.

Annie felt her pulse skip and she held her breath.

Claire barreled on, "Tourist season is winding down, but don't worry. These will also make wonderful gifts for all kinds of occasions."

"I hope so," Annie said, truly wondering about

Claire's flair for the dramatic. Would the paintings really sell? Time would tell.

"Especially Christmas," Claire added.

*Christmas.* The word squeezed Annie's heart. Months away yet, but the holidays would be strange without her father. And how terribly lonely if Ken faded from her life. The thought tangled in her chest.

Sadness washed over her. She'd done what she tried not to do—put hope in her relationship with Ken. Friendship was wonderful, but friendships weren't always lasting. He'd been a roamer. What would she do if he decided to move again? Or if he just faded from her life?

# *Chapter Fourteen*

"And Claire wants everything?" Ken glanced at Annie's bright eyes as they headed to the Père Marquette in Grand Haven.

Annie gave him a gentle pat. "I'm glad you've bugged me about painting again."

"Me? Bug you?" He wondered if she'd catch on to his meaning.

"Guilty as charged."

She had taken the comment good-naturedly. That pleased him. Annie had eased up a little, or as much as she could. Prodding seemed to be in his blood.

He saw the sign for the Grand Haven Historical Museum and turned into the harborfront parking lot.

As Ken stepped outside, a tickle dragged across his throat. He covered his mouth to cough. He hurried around the car to open Annie's door, surprised that she'd waited for him.

As she stepped out, she gave him a knowing grin. "See. I can be patient."

He laughed and amidst the pleasurable moment the same dryness caught in his throat, demanding another cough.

"You okay?" Annie asked.

"Must be something in the air," he said, waving off her concern.

They paused a moment to look for Jemma and Philip in the crowd across the street. Ken heard Jemma's voice and turned to see her heading his way. Philip followed with Ellie in his arms.

"Hello," Jemma called from a few cars away.

Annie waved and sent her a smile.

"Good to see you," Jemma said, reaching their side. "Glad you two could make it."

"Thanks for inviting us," Annie said.

Ken watched Philip arrive and noted that he was looking distracted. He wondered what was wrong. Something, for sure.

They waited for traffic to clear before crossing the street toward the museum, which had once been the train depot, and the Père Marquette steam locomotive that stood beside it. Heading for the train, they waited their turn as families wove their way in and out of the cars. Ken climbed aboard and gave Annie a hand, then Jemma. Philip made his own way and lowered Ellie to the train floor as they wandered through the caboose.

After wending their way to the engine, Philip let Ellie ding the bell. Ken watched Annie, mesmerized by her reaction to the child. Her eyes brightened and a smile lit her face as she bent down to speak to the toddler or tie her shoe before Jemma could.

He took his turn with Annie at his side, her laughter ringing in his ears. The sound of her laughter filled him with happiness, and though he hated crowds—strangers who might recognize him—today he pushed his fears aside.

After everyone had taken a turn at the bell, they climbed off the old steam engine and headed for the ice cream stand.

As they walked, Ken slid his arm around Annie's waist, enjoying the closeness and loving her comfortable smile. A crowd hovered around the stand while they waited.

Ellie stood beside her mother, hanging onto her pant leg, and Ken had a better look at Philip without the toddler in his arms. He seemed preoccupied, his hands deep in his pockets, a faraway look on his face. Jemma's gaze, also, seemed distracted.

The picture disturbed Ken. He had learned to care about Jemma and Philip and hated to see some unknown trouble causing them stress.

Annie had noticed, too, since her sidelong glance often took in both of them. Finally, she raised the question that Ken had longed to ask.

"Not feeling well, Philip?" Annie asked.

He jolted from his reverie. "Me? No. I'm fine."

Jemma shook her head. "No, he's not. He heard from Andrew."

Ken had no idea who Andrew was and neither did Annie from the look on her face.

Philip's shoulders drooped. "Andrew's my long-lost brother. The family prodigal."

*Prodigal.* The word punched Ken in the solar plexus. He'd been a prodigal. He held his breath waiting to hear if Philip would say more.

"You don't know my brother. He's been away for years," Philip said.

Jemma wove her fingers through Philip's. "I don't know him either. I've only seen photos, but he's as good-looking as Philip." With her free hand, she brushed her finger along her husband's tense jaw.

Philip captured Jemma's hand and lowered it, as if to stop her demonstration of concern. Then as if to make amends, he slid his arm around her and drew her nearer. "A long time ago Andrew took his share of the family business so he could live his own life. He wanted nothing to do with the resort. My father let him. He understood. I didn't."

"So he left the area?" Annie asked.

"He's been all over the place," Jemma said. "We get periodic telephone calls…like today."

Telephone calls. Ken knew what phone calls, or the lack of them, could do. So often in prison he'd waited, hoping to hear from his mother. Sometimes he was on the calling end, wondering why his mother—anyone—hadn't visited him.

"Andrew mentioned coming home…again. It's always talk. I wish he would," Philip said. "He didn't even come home for our father's funeral."

"You want him back?" Ken asked, surprised at Philip's attitude.

"From the bottom of my heart. We need to clear the air. To forgive. I forgave him long ago, but he doesn't believe it. He hears my frustration. I wish I could explain that my disappointment isn't about what he did or his leaving home. It's about his not coming back."

Ken weighed his words. *I forgave him long ago.* Forgiveness. Faith. Words that had never been a part of Ken's vocabulary. *It's not about…his leaving. It's about his not coming back.* The concept seemed beyond Ken's comprehension. Full forgiveness and more than that. Forgiveness with open arms. Like the picture of Jesus his mother had on her bedroom dresser.

"I'd give Andrew a welcome home party," Philip said, his words jarring Ken from his thoughts.

Jemma drew in a lengthy breath. "We're praying the day comes."

"Enough of my worries," Philip said, scooping Ellie into his arms. "Let's have some ice cream."

Filled with new thoughts, Ken studied Philip, wondering how he could so willingly forgive just as Annie had done. Philip had called his brother a prodigal. Hadn't he taken money from the family business and never returned—even for his father's funeral.

Maybe he hadn't. Ken didn't know the details, but he did know one important fact. Philip had a forgiving heart, and Ken needed a man to talk with.

One day, maybe he would.

\* \* \*

Annie stood in front of the mirror, winding her hair into a knot at the back of her neck. She attached the clip and stepped back to look at herself, turning from side to side. No straggles.

She recalled the day Ken had seen her hair hanging loose for a moment. His expression had surprised her, and he told her how much he'd like it hanging down. She wondered why she'd never worn it that way.

Ken had called before she left for work, suggesting they go out to dinner. But Annie was concerned. His voice sounded raspy, and she remembered his cough a couple days earlier. She feared he'd caught some kind of bug.

Annie turned back to the mirror to attach a pair of button earrings, then found her handbag and headed downstairs. Halfway down the telephone rang, and she hurried to catch it.

The voice that greeted her, though familiar, sounded awful. "Ken?"

"It's me," he croaked. "Sorry, but I'm going to cancel. I feel rotten."

Annie's concern shifted to guilt. The rainstorm. She pictured Ken standing in the torrential downpour to re-peg the tent...for her. "I'm so sorry. I'm sure you're sick from the storm at the art fair."

"That was days ago," he said through his congestion. He muffled a cough. "Don't worry about it."

"You sound terrible."

"I just need some rest."

"And chicken soup."

"I'm fine, Annie."

She wouldn't argue. "I'll be over in an hour or so."

"Please don't—"

"No more than two hours," she said and hung up before he could dissuade her.

Annie felt responsible, no matter what he said. Colds took time to develop, and he'd been so gallant that day. Annie opened the pantry closet and grabbed a can of chicken broth, then moved to the freezer for the chicken breasts.

Whether Ken wanted her to or not, she planned to nurse him back to health with the best medicine she knew, one she'd learned from her mother. Chicken soup.

In less than two hours, Annie had a container carefully wedged in the car so it wouldn't spill and was headed for Ken's. When she arrived, she clasped the covered bowl against her side and climbed the porch steps. She gave the knob a turn. It opened.

"Hello," she called.

A loud sneeze greeted her from the back of the house.

Annie dropped her shoulder bag on a living-room chair, then left the container in the kitchen and followed the hallway toward the sound. At the last doorway, she looked inside and saw Ken sprawled on the bed, covered by a quilt. The spread was dotted with tissues from a box that stood on the nightstand. Ken's face appeared flushed in the dim light, and when she neared him, his red nose seemed sore.

"You look horrible," she said. She grasped a

nearby wastebasket and began to toss away the soiled tissues.

"I'll be fine," he said, his congestion affecting the sound of his words.

When Annie finished straightening the bed, she washed her hands, then sat on the edge and pressed the back of her hand to his face. Heat sprang from his forehead and cheeks.

She stood. "Where's your thermometer?"

He shook his head. "I don't think I own one."

"Everyone has a thermometer." She pushed her fists against her hips and waited.

"Medicine cabinet."

She turned on her heel and marched across the hall into the bathroom. Opening the cabinet, she shuffled items around—deodorant, a can of bandage strips, razor blades, razor, toothbrush and paste—until finally she found a thermometer on the top shelf behind a tube of disinfectant.

Annie found alcohol and cleaned the thermometer, then checked the degrees and shook it down. She strode to the bedroom and shoved it beneath Ken's tongue before he had time to complain. He lay quietly.

Giving the thermometer a couple of minutes, Annie returned to the kitchen and filled a bowl with soup, then popped it into the microwave. She pressed the buttons and returned to the bedroom.

Checking his temperature, she gaped at the degrees. "A hundred and two," she said, shaking the numbers back to normal. "No wonder you feel rotten."

She slid the instrument into the storage case. "I want you to eat."

"I'm not hungry."

"I don't care. It's good for you. And you need aspirin."

A faint grin replaced his look of misery.

She left and returned with two tablets, a glass of water and a cool cloth. She took a moment to wipe the perspiration that beaded on his face and felt the stubble of beard on his jaw.

Ken caught her hand. "I guess you're going to be my nursemaid whether I want one or not."

"You got that right," she said, pulling away and hurrying to the kitchen. When she returned, she sat beside the bed, ladled some soup into the spoon, and held it toward his mouth.

Ken shook his head and pushed himself higher on the pillows. "If you're forcing me to eat, you can at least let me feed myself." He took the spoon and guided it to his mouth. "It's good, Annie."

"Thanks," she said.

"You're too good to me."

She ignored his comment and watched him shovel down some soup before accepting the nearly-empty bowl.

Ken fell back to his pillow, and Annie stepped back, watching him a moment. She loved the feeling of being the woman in his life. Caring for him, showing him how much he meant. Today the dark thoughts had left his eyes, replaced by fever. She wished those problems could vanish forever.

Annie tiptoed from the room and settled into a recliner in the living room. She rubbed her hand along
the chair arm, feeling the upholstery nap to regain
some sense of reality. She loved it here, caring for
Ken, making him soup and wiping his brow. She let
the feelings drift over her until time began to drag.
She found the newspaper and skimmed its pages, then
flipped through the TV channels until she found
something tolerable. Ken probably expected her to go
home, but she couldn't. She wanted to be with him.

Time passed at a snail's pace, and finally she
drifted down the hallway and leaned against the doorjamb. Ken lay on his side, his face to the wall. While
she watched, he rolled over and looked at her.

"Still here?" he asked.

"Mm-hmm."

He reached out and patted the edge of the bed.
"Come here."

Curious, she stepped closer, and his warm hand
caught hers.

"You don't have to stay here, Annie. It's just a
cold."

Annie studied his face, feeling relieved that he appeared less flushed. She touched his forehead, noticing it had cooled from a couple hours earlier. "Feeling better?" She stepped away, keeping him in her
vision, and headed for the thermometer.

"Much better." He swung his legs over the edge
of the mattress and rose. "I'm tired of this bed. I've
been here all day."

"Go into the living room, and I'll bring your pillow." She sent him on his way, then changed her course and gathered the bedding.

When she reached him, he was standing beside the sofa gazing across the room and through the bay window.

"You can't go out and play," she said, flashing him a playful smile. Annie propped the pillows and placed the quilt nearby.

Ken sent her a fabricated moan as she steered him toward the sofa. He stretched out, looking less glassy-eyed than earlier.

"I've never been treated so well," he said, his hands folded above his head.

"Sure you have."

"No. I haven't." His expression darkened like a growing storm.

She felt her eyes narrow and a frown tug at her mouth. "When you were a kid? Your mom certainly—"

"You don't understand, Annie. I wasn't allowed to be a kid." His voice cut with an unpleasant edge.

A mixture of intrigue and concern settled over her, and she remembered her promise not to bug him. "You're right. I don't understand."

His face washed with an eddy of emotion. Sorrow. Despair. Longing. "I'm sorry, Annie. It's this cold."

She knew it wasn't the cold, but she could only pray the truth would come out eventually. "I understand," she said, but she didn't. She didn't understand anymore than she comprehended the reason he kept his childhood so secret.

"I think I'll go and let you rest," she said, walking to the chair and picking up her shoulder bag.

A puzzled look spread across his face. "Sure," he said, a ring of concern in his voice. "Thanks for the soup and—"

"Don't forget to take a couple more aspirin," she said, backing toward the doorway.

Ken pulled himself up on one elbow and watched her through dazed eyes, knowing he should say something, but letting her go.

She gave a wave as she hurried out the door, and he fell back against the pillow. He was an utter jerk. As useless as a dead plant. As unworthy as mud. He was letting the only good thing in his life slip through his fingers because he was a coward.

*Be men of courage; be strong. Do everything in love.* The Bible verse sailed through his head. He'd fallen so short of that he could barely face himself, let alone Annie.

He pictured her standing at his side blotting his forehead with a cool cloth, plumping his pillow, trying to spoon-feed him. She gave and gave while he took and took, giving nothing in return. He didn't deserve the air she breathed.

His life revolved around his past, his years in prison where he'd felt hope and love shrivel. Now he had another chance. A door had opened and given him a chance to breathe again. Instead he'd stayed behind the bars of his fear, in a prison of his own making. And the only way he'd find freedom was through the truth. The truth could set him free.

Where had that thought come from? The answer struck him as quickly as the question. The Bible. Annie had aroused his interest. He'd asked himself over and over again how she could present the Lord as so loving when his father had taught him about an angry God who punished?

He was surprised Annie had persevered. He wondered if she thought he was a hopeless case. If so, her perception was close to correct. But her determination had made him see that there must be some truth to her prodding.

In past days, he'd been drawn to his mother's little red New Testament and had flipped through its pages, reading stories of healing. Rise up. Your faith has healed you. Wash in the river. Your faith has healed you. Awaken from the dead. Your faith has healed you.

*Faith.* The word had vaulted from the page. How could he deny the importance of faith? But where was his?

Ken rose, his legs unsteady. He headed for the bedroom and pulled his mother's New Testament from his nightstand drawer. On his way back to the living room, he stopped to take two more aspirin. As he swallowed, Annie's sweet face filled his thoughts. He owed her so much. In a way she didn't even know, Annie's purpose had been to set him free.

Back on the sofa, he opened the Bible and fingered through the pages. Where had he read that verse about being free? He'd been reading in the Book of St. John, he remembered. Focusing on the pages, he skimmed along the verses. St. John seven. St. John eight. He stopped when his eyes captured the words: Then said Jesus... If ye continue in my word, then are ye my disciples indeed; And ye shall know the truth, and the truth shall make you free.''

The words settled in Ken's heart. He feared the truth. He always had because it was *his* truth. Yet if he could forgive others, why not himself?

His gaze traveled farther along the page. Verily, verily, I say unto you, Whosoever commiteth sin is a servant of sin. Was he a slave to sin? His eyes followed the verse. If the Son therefore shall make you free, ye shall be free indeed.

Slave or prisoner? What was the difference? He'd enslaved himself to his secret. He'd let fear be the master...instead of God. When the Lord tried to step in and release him, he'd pushed Him away.

The truth will set you free. Truth and courage.

He needed so much to be worthy of Annie.

# Chapter Fifteen

Ken backed into Annie's driveway, wondering how things would go. Since she'd come to his house with the soup a couple days earlier, he realized he'd reacted badly. He'd been totally unthinking.

*Unthinking?* That was a misnomer. He wished he could be unthinking. All he'd done lately was think. Think about Annie. Think about himself. Think about God.

After shifting the truck into Park, he pushed open the door and stepped onto the driveway. The summer had offered the town cooler temperatures the past few days. Still warm but less humid. Rain had fallen, leaving the earth well-watered, and today the sky was clearer. In his work, he appreciated the gift.

He walked to the truck bed and pulled down the tailgate. He eyed Annie's shrubs, undisturbed by the ride.

He drew in a deep breath. Annie had been excited

when he'd called to say he'd be over to finish her new landscaping. He hoped the day would be more like old times when they'd sat on the porch and talked without all of the undertones of misunderstanding and riled emotions.

His wish stretched into a prayer, and the awareness settled over him in a comfortable stillness. Could this be how faith seeped into a person's life? Like air through pores? So minute, so subtle the individual was unaware?

Ken rang the bell, and before the last dong faded, Annie opened the front door. Seeing her took his breath away. How could he ever push this woman out of his life?

"Hi," he said. "Your landscaper's here and ready to work." Her sweet, spicy perfume drifted through the screen.

"Well it's about time." She gave him a teasing smile.

"Ready?"

She nodded. "I'll meet you out back."

Ken walked to the truck bed, lifted down a wheelbarrow and loaded on the balled shrubs. After he'd jostled it to the backyard, Annie came through the doorway. She stood on the stoop, watching as he pushed the barrow toward her, then stopped to pull her sketched plans from his pocket. He eyed them—out of proportion and unprofessional, but he loved her attempt.

Annie bounced down the steps, dressed in jeans

and a knit top, her hair in a rare ponytail, ready to be his helper, as she put it.

"Don't you look cute," he said, knowing she'd forgiven him for his bad behavior. He tugged off his work glove and caught her by the waist, drawing her close to his side.

"Don't get me dirty," she said, grinning as if she didn't mean one word.

He kissed the top of her head, her hair shimmering in the sunlight, then ran his fingers through the ponytail. He longed to pull out the elastic and let it fall in a golden stream around her shoulders. He'd only seen it down once. That day, his imagination had flown, picturing her in his arms, her pale golden hair, hiding its wisps of gray, spread out on a satin pillow.

He loved her smile. The last time he'd seen her she'd been frowning and angry, and it had been his fault.

"Sorry about the other day when I was so—"

"You were feeling rotten. Please don't apologize." She brushed her hand along his cheek, the caress warm and smooth.

"And now...let's get busy," she said.

Her quick switch from tenderness to business made him chuckle, and he grabbed the wheelbarrow handles and rolled the weighty burden across the lawn to the location Annie had chosen, a spot filled with sunshine.

Digging was easy after the rain, and each spadeful sent the aroma of warm earth into the air. He dropped the balled roots into the hole while Annie hovered by, chattering and bossing, just the way he loved her to be.

She helped him open the bags of peat and top soil, and while he poured, she shifted the fresh dirt with the shovel. Then he dragged the hose across the lawn to water. When the three new viburnums stood in a wide, straight line along the garden beds, he stepped back and swung his arm in a wide gesture. "What do you think?"

"We do good work," she said.

His gaze drifted to the new flower beds he'd already put into place. In a spaded circle, he'd planted flowers around a large birdbath. All Annie's idea. Beneath the large oak, he'd positioned the new garden bench.

"Let's sit," he said, needing a break before tackling the other shrubs. He dropped his work gloves into the wheelbarrow, then grabbed her hand.

"You'd be able to relax in the gazebo had you let me buy one," she said, her voice teasing. "Or, at least, the swing."

"The bench is nicer," he said, "and anyway, you already own a swing. A bench doesn't need oiling."

She laughed and tugged at his hand, guiding him toward the bench. The air shimmered with sunshine and flowers, and Ken felt as close to free as he'd felt since he was eighteen.

"You're a handsome man," Annie said, tilting her head to avoid the lowering sun.

"What?"

"I figured it's time I admit something that I've thought for a long time."

"You have." He wasn't used to hearing compliments and it left him feeling uneasy. Still he loved her admission. "Thank you. Should I be open, too?" he asked, surprised to hear his offer.

"I'd like that."

"You're a beautiful women. Every part of you. I'd love to pull that elastic from around your ponytail and run my fingers through your hair. I'd love to kiss these lovely lips," he said, brushing his finger along the curve of her mouth, then capturing her chin in his hand as he looked into her willing eyes.

As fearful as it had always been, love washed over him like a welcoming fire on a winter day. He lowered his lips to hers, tasting the sweet flavor of her mouth and drinking in the pleasure of her giving.

With his mouth moving with hers, longing rolled through him, yearning to have a life with her, wanting to be her husband, hungering to open his heart and soul to the love she offered him.

When he eased back, Annie's eyes opened slowly like the petals of a flower. Her sigh filled his heart, and he knew what he had to do.

He wasn't ready to lay everything in the open, but he needed to tell her how she'd changed his life. He slid his arm around her back, and she rested her head on his shoulder. They sat in silence a moment until he'd gathered his thoughts.

"I have to thank you for so much, Annie." He felt her stir but pulled her closer and continued, "You've encouraged me out of a closed world. You've helped me look at something other than my work…and you've made me think.''

She lifted her head. ''Think?''

Her perfume wrapped around him, the sweetness so like Annie herself. ''Think about faith. About God.''

She reached over and touched his arm. ''Hearing you say you're thinking means more to me than anything. If I've done that, I'm happy.''

''You've done more than that. It's harder for a man to put things into words than a woman, especially a man like me. Remember, I grew up in a home where feelings and wants weren't talked about.''

He caught her frown and stopped.

''I know, Ken, and I'm sorry for that.''

''No need. It wasn't your doing. You came out of your life better than I did. You win hands down.'' Thinking of the difficulties in both their lives, Ken felt ashamed he hadn't handled his better. His own youthful rebellion had been his undoing.

''Hands down nothing,'' Annie said. ''You're a winner. You just don't see yourself that way.'' She shifted to face him and brushed his arm with her fingertips. ''If this is confession time, I've been doing some serious thinking, too.''

Her words startled him, and he held his breath. Had the time finally come when she'd realized how undeserving he was to hold her in his arms, to kiss her as he had done?

She looked at him as if sensing his fear. "This has nothing to do with you and me."

He breathed again, now puzzled where she was headed.

"It has to do with my life. Talk about bringing someone out. You've done the same for me. I lived in my parents' house under the guise of caring for my father. That part was the truth, but I finally realized something so important, and it's taken me so long to realize it."

Her words surged through him, and he was curious about what was so important to her.

"I've been hiding much of my life," she said.

Her confession startled him. "What do you mean?"

"Hiding behind my parents' needs so I didn't have to deal with my own life. I don't know why, but I didn't seem to have a big crowd of friends. Maybe I pushed people away, afraid of being rejected. I don't know."

"Annie, I can't imagine that."

"Neither can I, Ken, but I think it's the truth." She shifted farther on the bench and knotted her hands in her lap. "I was comfortable caring for my family. I didn't have to explain why I had no social life, because I had a ready answer. As Susan and Donna said, I chose to be there."

"Annie, please—"

"No. This is important. Even you gave me a million suggestions on getting help for my father. I pushed the ideas away, because if I released control,

I'd have to get out and live. I enjoyed being a martyr."

Ken didn't want to hear her say those things. "I don't agree with you, Annie."

"It doesn't matter if you agree or not. It's the truth...and by admitting the truth, I'm free of it."

*Free of it.* Hadn't he just said the same thing about himself?

Ken ran his hand along her hair to the end of her ponytail, swallowing the words he wanted to say. He longed to tell her he loved her. *Friendship* didn't dent the feelings he had. Instead, he said nothing. He let his hand drop and grasped her fingers in his, wanting so badly to find the courage to finish his confession.

Annie watched the scenery flash past the window as they drove along the water, the sun glinting like jewels on the waves that rolled in aqua corrugations to the shore. She rolled down the window a moment and drew in the lake air.

"I'm glad you called," Annie said. "I hate spending my whole Saturday doing housework. I'd much rather get outside and enjoy the weather."

He gave her a quick smile, then turned his eyes back to the road.

She studied his tanned profile, his strong features looking more relaxed since they'd talked the other day about his faith and her martyrdom. Once it was in the open, she could get rid of the guilt. Free herself from the pressures.

In the distance, Annie could see the old Loving

Light rising from the edge of what now had become a park. She loved the old building for its history and its purpose. For years, it had stood, sending its beam across the black water to guide the sailors to safety. Like God, she thought.

"Let's stop at the park," she said, pointing toward the lighthouse.

"I figured we'd find a place to eat along the highway," he said.

"Later, okay? I'd really like to stop."

He reached across the space and gave her arm a pat. "No problem."

He pulled into an open space, and turned off the ignition. They exited the car, and Ken caught her hand in his.

"Great old lighthouse," he said.

"It's a shame they built the new one. All automated. No lighthouse keeper to fill a woman's mind with romance."

Ken chuckled. "I doubt if living in one of those things was very romantic for anyone—the keeper or his family."

"I know, but think of all the stories about storms and rescues."

He drew her closer, and his laugh filled her heart.

"Annie, I've never heard you this way before. Makes me want to be a swashbuckler."

She pulled away and ran ahead, feeling younger than her forty-three years. She headed toward a bench along the water's edge, and Ken followed, feeling a strange sense of freedom.

Annie stretched her legs out in front of her, feeling the sun's heat against her skin. "You know why a lighthouse has such a strong meaning to me?" Annie asked.

Ken shook his head. "No idea."

She looked toward the opening where the large lens had once been. "It reminds me of God's Word. Jesus is the light of the world. The light can keep people safe and rescue a drowning soul. It's poetic almost." She turned to face him. "But it's not poetry. It's in the Bible."

"The Bible…"

The two words made Annie stop. He didn't continue but let the thought hang on the air, anguish writhing on his face. She sensed it coming—the story she so longed to hear.

# Chapter Sixteen

Ken didn't look at her but toward the lake rolling to shore in ripples of aqua and sunshine, his face contorted with emotion.

"The Bible frightened me...until you came along," he said. "You hold it in reverence. You talk about its poetry and beauty. That was all foreign to me."

"Because of your father?"

"My father called himself a man of faith. I call him a religious fanatic. My mother was a quiet, humble woman, and I watched her be browbeaten by my father in the name of religion."

Annie cringed with his description.

He silenced, and they sat for a moment listening to the sound of the rolling waves against the shore and the squawk of a seagull.

Ken drew his shoulders upward and took a deep breath. "My father always carried a large, black leather Bible. Sometimes he read it aloud to us, stories about God's wrath and punishment.'' He flinched. ''Other times he used it to whack me across the head or beat me across my back. My mother never interfered. She'd learned her lesson well.''

''Oh, Ken, please—''

''You wanted to know about this. Hear me out.'' Ken arched his back and rubbed his hand across the nape of his neck, then fell against the bench. ''*Spare the rod and spoil the child.* That was my father's motto. Never forgiveness or understanding. Just pay for your mistake or sin.''

Annie thought of Proverbs and the many verses that taught about discipline and punishment. Grief filled her as she looked at Ken's face.

''He nearly broke my eardrum with that book. I remember the pain. I got an infection and I'll never forget the oozing and soreness.'' He closed his eyes and reached up to rub the spot beside his ear.

When Ken lowered his hand to his chest, he clasped his fingers together, resting his elbows on his knees, his gaze downward. ''When I got older and did anything not to his liking, my father would give me a punch and say I was getting what I deserved.''

''Did you ever strike back?'' Annie asked, unable to comprehend what Ken had endured. Her father's neglect seemed a gift compared to what she was hearing.

''Never. I couldn't do that. But I wanted to. If God punishes us for our thoughts, I'm a dead man.''

''I can't imagine what you've been through. I

thought Pa had problems, but he wasn't a mean drunk, just a drunk and a wastrel.''

"Dad penny-pinched, too. I had one pair of shoes that lasted me as long as I could still walk in them. No money for candy. My mother would sneak a treat once in a while, then live in fear that my father would check the grocery bill or notice the few extra dollars missing.''

"He hit your mother?''

Ken shook his head. "I never saw it, but she cowered so much that I imagine he did until I came along. If they'd had another child, maybe I'd have gotten off the hook.''

The bitterness in his voice knotted in Annie's chest. Sorrow. Hurt. Anger. All of them boiled inside her.

"And I learned well, Annie,'' he said, looking directly into her eyes for the first time since he'd begun talking. "You remember Henley's story about third grade? When I was a child, I didn't know how to talk with other kids. My reaction was to strike out or threaten when I ran into trouble. A punch or a fist fight. I was a terror. If I ever run into any more people from my past, I'm sure they'll have similar stories.''

Annie's stomach knotted as she listened. She couldn't imagine his pain. She ran her palm along his arm, feeling the tension that knotted the sinew in his limb.

"When I got old enough to rebel, I did,'' he said. "I sneaked behind my parents' backs, smoking, drinking, stealing.'' He waved his hand through the air and fell silent.

Finally he looked at her. "That's enough about me. You can see why the Bible hasn't always had pleasant memories and why church has been my enemy."

"I can't even imagine." She slipped her fingers through his and raised his hand to her lips, her mind whirring with all he'd said. "I'm amazed you kept your mother's New Testament all these years."

"My mother." He drew in a ragged breath and shook his head. "I can't talk about her, Annie. It kills me. Now that I'm older and remember how she lived, the fear in her eyes and the heartache she must have felt, it hurts too much."

He rose and Annie followed. They walked slowly along the path toward the parking lot. She brushed her fingers along Ken's arm, seeing the longing in his eyes and determination in his face.

The cleft in his chin winked as he tensed his jaw. She looked over her shoulder for another glimpse of the lighthouse standing tall, like a sentry, against the sky. She had no way to mend his wounds. Only God could do that.

As if hearing her thoughts, Ken squeezed her hand. "You're a good woman, Annie. A great woman."

She managed a pleasant smile.

"I'd like to go to church with you tomorrow."

She couldn't respond. She only nodded. Tears pushed against her eyes and emotions caught in her throat. All she could do was praise God for Ken's willingness to take a single step toward healing.

Annie climbed from Ken's car, still surprised, yet pleased that he'd asked to join her for worship. As he closed the passenger door, the church bells began to ring, and Annie slipped her fingers between his offered hand as they ascended the church steps.

She remembered the first time Ken had come to worship. He'd slipped in the back, and he might never have told her he'd been there except she'd seen him. Her mind rolled, reviewing what might have caused the change.

Annie stopped herself. It didn't matter. He was here. Then, as if God wanted her to know the answer, she stepped to the sanctuary doorway, and her questions ended.

In front of her, the sun beamed through the center stained-glass window—the cross between the descending dove and the eye of God. The Holy Spirit had made the difference and had opened Ken's heart to the Word. The answer seemed as simple as that.

Inside the sanctuary, Annie sat farther back than usual, thinking Ken would be more comfortable. Though he rose for the opening hymn, he didn't open the hymn book and during the Bible readings, his hands lay clenched in his lap.

Annie's heart ached for the torment that rocked Ken's spirit. Wanting to do something, she slipped her hand over his. He glanced down and wrapped his fingers through hers.

When the pastor spoke, Annie tried to stay focused on the Word as his voice lifted with the reading.

From Second Corinthians, he said, *"Rather, we have renounced secret and shameful ways; we do not use deception, nor do we distort the word of God. On the contrary, by setting forth the truth plainly we commend ourselves to every man's conscience in the sight of God.''*

Ken's fingers tightened around hers. Annie saw him lean forward as if concentrating on the lesson. Her pulse tripped, praying that the Word had touched his heart.

He'd told her about his past, but he needed to let it go. She paused in her reverie. Or had there been more? Had something else happened to Ken to cause him such untold sorrow? His broken engagement to Cheryl? Could that be it?

The pastor continued by speaking of God's abounding forgiveness and mercy to those who called on His name. Annie winced, knowing she had so often forgotten to ask God for help. So often bungled on alone.

As the Word wrapped around her, she rejoiced with the message. In the quiet church, she bowed her head in silent prayer for forgiveness for her wrongdoings. As the words left Annie, her anger at her siblings, her personal frustration and the guilt for probing Ken with questions rolled away. She was truly sorry and felt truly forgiven.

Ken's hand relaxed in hers. She looked over to study his face. The stress had eased, and his taut jaw had softened. When he glanced her way, his eyes seemed brighter, and he sent her a shy smile.

Annie squeezed his hand, sensing something important had happened. When the service ended, they followed the others outside, and she promised herself not to ask, not to pry, and not to hope too much. She would put it in God's hands, where it belonged.

Ken patted her arm. "Could you wait a minute? I need to catch Philip." He hurried away while Annie watched him go, curious what he had to say to Philip.

He took long strides to reach Philip's side before anyone else did.

"Ken," Philip said, extending his hand. "Great to see you here again."

"Thanks," Ken said, shaking his hand, but without warning, his confidence faded. "I wondered if, well, you mentioned pulling out some of those overgrown shrubs, and I wondered if I could drop by to talk about which ones and what you want as replacements."

"Sure, but I can leave it to your judgment. You're the landscaper."

"I know, but I prefer to check things out with you."

Philip nodded as if he understood. "How about dropping by this afternoon? Or we could make it Monday."

Tension rose up Ken's neck and he was sorry he'd charged over with his feeble cover-up story. He'd wanted to talk with Philip about himself. His life and how forgiveness fit in, but he'd acted in desperation, and what he needed was composure and reason.

"Which is best for you?" Ken asked.

"This afternoon's good, but I don't suppose you want to work on Sunday."

"Today's fine. About two?"

"Two's great," Philip said.

Ken said goodbye, then returned to Annie, feeling disappointed in himself. He'd never burdened anyone other than Annie with his problems. What did he expect from Philip? He wasn't sure, but something inside nudged him forward. As he passed the sanctuary door, his gaze caught the window above the altar.

The cross, the dove and the eye of God.

Annie sat at her easel, catching the afternoon sun. On Sundays, the street was quiet and she had opened the window to enjoy the soft breeze. With September just around the corner, she could already breathe in the rich scent of decaying leaves. A few had already faded to a dull pea-soup green and, in a couple more weeks, they would turn gold.

Looking in the mirror that morning after church, she'd noticed a few gray hairs nestled among her blond ones. Gray hair. The thought flattened her spirit. She wasn't afraid to grow old, but she'd longed for so many things before that day. Things she might never have.

She lifted a fine-tipped brush and created the slender petals of a flower. Pink on white on pink, yellow on white, highlighted to give a hint of sunlight. She changed the brush and daubed it with umber and forest green, adding shadow to the grass beneath the flowers.

Although she sat alone with her paints, today seemed special. Ken sitting beside her during worship had uplifted her and given her hope. His tensed fingers had relaxed, his taut jaw eased. She'd hoped somehow God would open his eyes to forgiveness. Yet she couldn't blame him for his anger.

Imagining his past aroused her curiosity. How had Ken come from those roots with a tender heart and gentle loving ways? Only the Lord could understand how those things happened. She looked at her own life. Once she'd thought she'd had it bad, but recalling Ken's story, she knew her problems had been nothing.

Again she pondered Ken's conversation with Philip. What business did he have? Something about the landscaping, she was certain. But why on Sunday afternoon? Annie pushed aside her thoughts and concentrated on her watercolors.

Claire had told her last week she'd sold three of Annie's paintings. Though Annie still had others to sell, she'd need to keep her stock replenished. For so long, painting had filled many lonely nights, but today, her painting had a new purpose and gave her fresh energy.

With a final stroke, Annie leaned back to take a critical look. She never quite saw what others did in her work. She thought they looked good because she'd painted them. Now she tried to see them through others' eyes. It was like life—trying to understand it through another person's eyes. As she set down the brush, the telephone's jingle caused her to jump.

Ken, she hoped.

Annie wiped her hands and scooted to the kitchen phone. Disappointment rolled through her when she heard the greeting on the other end of the line. She swallowed and responded, "Susan, how are you?"

"Great," her sister said, her voice syrupy sweet. "I just came back from visiting Carol in Fremont."

Something in her tone sent chills along Annie's back. "How is Carol?"

"Fine. Doing very well."

"And the kids?"

"They're good."

Annie waited for the bomb to drop.

"I'm not sure if I should tell you this, Annie," Susan's voice had picked up an edge of artificial distress blending with her saccharin pleasantness.

The paradox struck Annie with fear. "Tell me what?"

"What I learned in Fremont...from Carol."

Annie paused and tried to calm her voice. "I'm a big girl, Susan. Just say it."

"It's about Ken."

# Chapter Seventeen

*Ken.* The name hit Annie's heart like a bullet, and icy tendrils snaked through her limbs. "What about Ken?" she asked, her hand beginning to shake against the receiver.

"He's an ex-con. He was in prison for several years," Susan said, her attempt at distress now faded to pure malice.

"Prison?" Annie said, keeping her voice steady. Her knees weakened, and she grasped a chair and drew it closer to the phone. "Ken Dewitt?" Her sister had to be wrong. Annie eased her trembling body into the chair. Another Ken. Another Dewitt, but not her gentle friend who'd been so kind.

"Carol's positive. Ken Dewitt had been engaged to one of her friends. Cheryl Wilkes. Carol told me that shortly before the wedding Cheryl learned about it and broke off the engagement. He didn't take it well from what I heard. He's a violent man...but then you probably have witnessed that yourself by now.''

Annie couldn't speak. Cheryl. Yes, Ken had mentioned Cheryl. She drew in a ragged breath. Cheryl, maybe, but violent? Never. ''No, Susan. If it's the same Ken Dewitt, he's changed.''

''No one really changes, Annie. You're too gullible.''

''I'll keep that in mind.'' Her hand quavered as she pressed the receiver to her ear. Annie wanted to escape. To hang up. To erase her message like an answering machine and go back to minutes earlier. She wouldn't have answered the telephone. But it was too late.

Silence stretched into uncomfortable seconds.

''Are you still seeing him?'' Susan asked, her question ringing with doom.

''Yes.''

Annie heard her sister's intake of breath.

''Well then...what will you do now?'' Her tone had shifted to the familiar businesswoman of her last visit.

''Nothing,'' Annie said, without thinking.

''Nothing? Are you crazy?''

''Do you have to ask? I've stayed on the telephone without hanging up on you. I must be.''

The slam of the receiver rang in Annie's ears. She hung her head as sobs raked her body. Guilt. Sorrow. Fear wrapped around her heart. She grasped for threads of wisdom.

She'd sensed that Ken had more to tell. His grief

seemed deeper than the childhood abuse he'd told her about. His reserve. His withdrawal from strangers. The moving from place to place he'd mentioned. But prison? Violence? She hadn't even asked the crime. Assault and battery? Robbery?

Murder?

Ken left his car parked in the street and headed up Philip's sidewalk. Before he reached the porch, Philip opened the door and stepped out to the brick entry.

"Is this a good time for you?" Ken asked as he approached.

"Perfect. Ellie's napping and Jemma has some sewing to do."

"Good." He gestured toward the shrubbery beneath the bay window. "Let's check things in front," Ken said, "before we go to the back."

Philip agreed and followed Ken to the edge of the property. As they walked along discussing shrubbery and trees, Ken took notes on his clipboard while his inner thoughts dwelt on his personal struggles.

The decisions fell together quickly, and when they moved to the backyard, Philip suggested they take a break. While he went inside to grab some drinks, Ken weighed his need to be candid with Philip. To talk about things he'd discussed with no one.

Why Philip? he asked himself. The answer seemed easy. Philip had forgiven his brother for many transgressions. Maybe he would have enough compassion to hear Ken's story without turning against him.

Ken balked at his thoughts. He'd stood on his own

feet since he was eighteen. He'd needed no one. Fact was, he had no one. He'd become a loner. A man of few words. A man who avoided strangers rather than face another fiasco.

The screen door slammed, and Philip crossed the lawn carrying two cans of soda. He handed one to Ken, then motioned him toward the chairs on their fieldstone patio.

"Let's sit," Philip said. "We can talk about the yard in general before we get into specifics." He gave Ken a crooked smile.

Ken managed a smile and sank into a nearby chair. He took a sip of the cold beverage, letting the moisture spread over his parched throat.

Setting his can down on the umbrella table, Philip let his gaze travel the length of the yard. He addressed some shrubs that needed removal and his thoughts on a flowering tree he'd been considering.

Ken took notes, adding his comments as they talked.

When a lull came, Philip leaned back a moment and eyed Ken. "You're a good man, Ken, but I sense your mind is only half on this job. What's troubling you?"

He'd caught Ken off guard, and Ken rambled a moment, trying to recover. Finally he settled on the truth. "I've wondered how you were able to forgive your brother."

Philip rubbed the back of his neck a moment before answering. "It didn't happen that day or the next week. In fact, forgiveness was slow to come." He stared into space. "The opposite of our Lord who is slow to anger and plenteous in mercy. Mercy took a long time in coming." He turned back to Ken without asking questions. He only studied Ken's face.

Ken's pulse escalated and his breathing came short. "I've struggled with things, awful things, in my life and haven't quite made the step."

"Do you want to talk?" Philip asked.

Ken weighed his words. Did he want to talk? Yes. No. The pendulum swung in both directions. If he opened his bag of transgressions, would he have to run again?

"You don't have to," Philip said in response to his silence. "I understand. Confession is difficult."

Ken could only nod, frozen in anxiety and speculation.

Philip began again. "After Andrew left, I was happy he'd gone. He'd been a stumbling block to my dad and to the business. Nothing but hassles. I look back on it now and see it differently."

Ken's face must have triggered the need for an explanation because Philip continued, "He wanted to go away and to do his own thing, be his own person. That's how he put it, but the only way he had the strength to leave was to create enough dissension to make his leaving a relief. Sort of asking our father to tell him to get out—but he didn't."

Ken understood. "I suppose that's what I've been doing to Annie."

"Giving her reason to push you away?"

Ken nodded. "She's a wonderful woman and needs a good solid man to love her."

"And you're not good and solid?"

Ken looked at him and shrugged. "I try to be."

"Then what's the problem?"

"I wasn't always. I made big mistakes in my life. Mistakes I can hardly talk about."

Philip nodded as if he understood. "We've all made them."

"No. I don't think so."

Ken began slowly, avoiding his prison sentence, but talking about his engagement and Cheryl's rejection when he confessed his sinful past. He admitted his deep feelings for Annie.

Philip's face remained calm, unmoved, except to show a gentle understanding of Ken's sorrow. "Was your sin beyond forgiveness?" Philip asked.

"For Cheryl it was."

"But would it be for Annie?"

Ken drew in a lengthy breath. "I don't know."

"Annie is a good woman. You said it yourself. She took care of her father, dealt with her siblings through that ordeal. You know. You were there. She's compassionate. Understanding. Loving. I can't believe that you could say anything to have her turn her back on you," Philip said.

Ken faced him. "I love her."

"I know you do…and she loves you. It's obvious."

Annie loved him. Could that be true? He'd blinded himself to so many emotions while struggling with his pitiful preoccupation with his past. "She loves me?"

Philip grinned. "I'd bet my last dollar."

If Annie loved him, Ken needed to test the water. Test Philip to see how he would react to Ken's past violence, his prison term. He began and the words spilled out of him like matter from an opened abscess, cleansing the wound that had ached for so many years.

Philip didn't blanch. Instead, he leaned closer, nodded as if he understood and when Ken had finished, he looked at Ken with caring eyes and thanked him for sharing his story. "Your past has been more difficult than I can even imagine. The present, rough, living with the guilt. Don't take it into the future, Ken. Let God carry your burden. Let Annie's love do the rest."

Drained, Ken clasped his quaking hands against his belly and controlled his voice enough to say thank you. His mind filled with Annie. He should have told her long ago. And he would today.

# Chapter Eighteen

Annie punched in the buttons and listened to the telephone ring. She'd struggled with her decisions to call Carol or to ignore Susan's comments and see them as bitter retaliation. But despite her meanness, Susan had to have spoken some kind of truth, and Annie needed to know.

When she heard Carol's voice, Annie's heart fell to her stomach. Nausea rolled through her and sent a burning sensation into her throat. She swallowed the acrid fire. "Carol. Hi. This is Annie."

"Annie. It's so good to hear your voice. I'm sorry about your dad. How are you doing?"

Her behavior seemed as normal as usual and Annie stared into space, puzzled. "I'm okay. I miss Pa, despite all the hard times we had."

"I can imagine," Carol said. "Even a grouchy old man is better than empty rooms."

Annie didn't need to explain or comment. She had

her purpose for calling. "Carol, Susan called me today."

"Oh...I figured. She sounded gleeful. Do you know Ken Dewitt?"

"I thought she'd told you," Annie said, wondering what Susan had related. "Ken has been a good friend through all the difficult times with Pa. I just can't believe—"

"I shouldn't have said anything to Susan, Annie. I'm sorry."

"Tell me what really happened," Annie said.

Carol began and related much the same story that Susan had told her—the prison term and the broken engagement.

"Susan said he was violent. I've never seen that in him. Never."

"I don't think I said violent. Apparently he was arrested for breaking and entering. He'd done a lot of damage to a woman's house. At least that's what Cheryl told me."

Breaking and entering. Damage. Annie couldn't speak. She pictured the gentle man who'd helped her father up from the floor, who'd stood by her side when her father was taken to emergency, who'd defended her when her sisters had acted so horribly, who'd held her in his arms and kissed away her tears.

"I can't envision it," Annie said. "He's been nothing but kind and gentle. He's encouraged me to get on with my life, to get a job, to sell my watercolors. I'm shocked."

"I'm sorry, Annie. That's what I've heard. I didn't

know him myself. It all happened before he came to Fremont.''

Though Carol tried to ease the news, Annie still felt the sting of the revelation. Why hadn't Ken told her? When he'd talked about his childhood, why hadn't he gone ahead to tell her about his adult years?

"He's probably changed," Carol added, filling the silence.

"Yes, he has, I guess," Annie said.

She thanked her cousin and hung up the telephone, drained and heartbroken. Ken didn't trust her enough to tell her the truth.

And was that all the truth or was there more?

Ken pulled away from Philip's and drove toward Annie's. While he had the courage, he had to tell her the story. No matter what happened. She'd trusted him with her friendship and so much more. He owed her the truth even if it meant goodbye.

His heart ached. For the first time in many years, he'd allowed himself to taste love, to imagine himself as a married man, to think of holding a woman in his arms. He'd blocked those feelings, hiding behind his work and his silence. What would he do now that he'd opened the door to his emotions?

Anger filled him. Anger for the past. Anger for the present. But the future... The future? He had no answer until he talked with Annie.

Before he neared her street, he pulled off and found an empty space at the city park. He left the car and wandered to the fountain. He watched the water wash over the curved concrete and splash into the basin. For years, the water had smoothed the rough edges. Had life smoothed his? He felt his eyes brim with moisture.

Tears. He hadn't shed tears since he was an infant. And why tears? Pity? Fear? Yes, both. Pity for his useless life and fear of losing Annie.

Words filled his mind. Annie's words. *The end of the verse is my favorite. Want to hear it?* She remembered it perfectly. He'd checked later, reading it over and over. *And now these three remain: faith, hope and love. But the greatest of these is love.*

Sweet Annie. Her loving ways embraced him. Hope filled him. Hope and love. Hope that Annie would understand. Love for the woman who'd revitalized his life. Faith? He was working on that. One day faith would come, he prayed. Unquestioning faith.

Calming his ragged thoughts, Ken returned to his car and drove the rest of the way to Annie's. Arriving, he took a deep breath before making his way up the porch stairs. The doorbell jangled his stress-filled nerves. He waited, holding his breath.

When Annie opened the door, her face paled, and she stood there without speaking.

Something had happened. Something awful.

"Ken. I wasn't expecting you." Her words were strained.

"I need to talk with you."

"And I need to talk with you, but not now."

She clung to the door, and he sensed something had happened. Things had changed.

"What's wrong?" Ken asked, keeping his hand from clasping the screen door handle.

"My sister called today."

Blessed relief washed over him. Susan. The cause of her stress. "What happened?" He gave the screen door a tug and found it locked.

Annie didn't budge. "She'd just come home from visiting our cousin in Fremont."

The look in her eyes told the story. He needed no more information. "Annie, I'm sorry. I came here today to tell you what I should have told you long ago."

"You don't have to. I heard."

"But I wanted to explain how—" He stared at her through the screen.

"Ken, I need to think. I'm shocked. Hurt that you let this go on without talking with me. I'm speechless at what I've heard today." She pressed her fist against her heart, her eyes pinning him to the door frame. "In prison for several years and you didn't say a word."

Tears filled her eyes as panic filled Ken's mind. He saw an instant replay of years earlier. Cheryl backing away. Withdrawing. Pushing out her hands to block his steps toward her. Nothing had changed. Annie's capacity to understand was no greater than Cheryl's. Her willingness to hear his story as empty. The hurt and disappointment jarred his being.

He staggered backward, fighting to control his own tears. "I made a mistake, Annie." A mistake. A mistake to trust again. A mistake to think Annie was different. He reeled with hopelessness. "I'm sorry."

"I can't see you now," she said, taking steps backward as she pushed the door shut. "I need to think."

He watched the door closing in his face. Annie's gray eyes as angry and misted as a storm-filled sky. He turned and ran down the steps.

Ran as he'd done so often.

Annie gathered toys and tossed them into the basket. As she worked, she kept her eye on Ellie. This was Jemma's day to relax by leaving her toddler at Loving Care. Annie enjoyed the child, and today she hugged her more than usual, feeling the tremendous loss of Ken's friendship.

Nearly a week had passed since Ken had walked out of her life, run from it. But the truth was she had pushed him away. She'd literally closed the door in his face.

The look in his eyes tore at her day and night. The image rose in her thoughts like a specter, haunting her every moment, and she'd struggled with her actions. Had she reacted with compassion and love? Had she acted like a Christian?

Disappointment had pressed against her heart. The news had smothered her sensibility. Lost and abandoned, she sat staring at the phone, longing for his call, wanting to call him, but hurt and pride had stopped her.

*Pride goeth before the fall.* The words ripped through her mind. Her mother's words. The Bible's message. Annie had tried to think. Tried to weigh the possibilities of why Ken had done those horrible things. Then, why he hadn't told her? The questions seemed paradoxical. Yet both pressed on her mind like a gravestone.

"You can go," Christie said.

Annie jumped at her voice. Her hand clutched at her pounding heart.

"Sorry. I didn't mean to scare you," Christie said. "You've been terribly thoughtful. Something wrong?"

Annie pressed her lips together, afraid she'd let her thoughts loose. If she did only one good thing, she'd promised herself to keep Ken's secret.

"I guess I'm not feeling well," Annie said, to cover the truth. Yet in truth, she felt horrible.

"Take tomorrow off, Annie. I'll manage."

Christie's offer touched Annie. "I'll feel better by then, I'm sure." If she didn't, she needed to keep a smile on her face and her mind focused on the kids.

Ellie waddled across the floor and clung to Annie's pant leg. She bent and lifted the child in her arms, giving her another kiss on the cheek. How many that made for this day, Annie had no idea. "Your mama will be here soon, Ellie."

"Mama," Ellie said.

Annie nodded.

Her nod was followed by Ellie's squeal. "Mama!"

Annie swung around and saw Jemma in the doorway. Jemma opened her arms, and Annie lowered Ellie to the ground.

The tot hurried across the room on chubby legs to her mother. The greeting caught Annie's emotions. She felt foolish, allowing tears to fill her eyes at the sight of mother and child.

Jemma raised her hand in greeting to Annie, but her smile faded when she looked at Annie's face.

Annie turned away to brush the moisture from her eyes. Bending down, she pulled another toy from the floor and dropped it into the basket, then turned again to face Jemma.

"She was an angel today as always," Annie said, managing to brighten her voice.

Jemma moved closer. "But what about you? Something's wrong."

Annie shrugged, unable to speak with her heart knotted in her throat.

"Are you finished for the day?" Jemma asked.

Annie gave a faint nod. "I'm fine. Really."

"Good," Jemma said, her voice assuring Annie that she hadn't been fooled. "How about some coffee? Do you have time?"

Time. That's all Annie had. "Right now, you mean?"

"Sure. How about the coffee shop up the road? Dee's Café."

"Okay," Annie said, wondering what she could say to Jemma that wouldn't break Ken's confidence.

While Jemma chased Ellie, who'd decided to run and hide, Annie pulled her purse from the storage cabinet and threw her sweater over her arm.

Jemma captured the child, then gave a wave as she

left, and Annie said good-night to Christie, apologizing for her lethargy.

"Hope you feel better tomorrow," Christie called.

Annie hoped the same.

Inside her car, Annie sat a moment, gathering her thoughts. As she'd done for days, she reviewed the pros and cons of Ken's attributes and found no cons, only his melancholy and restrained manner. But now that she'd learned the truth, she understood. He'd been hurt and lived in fear of discovery.

She added Ken's upbringing—his father's misunderstanding of God's Word and his mother's inability to help him change. Sadness washed over Annie like a torrent.

Now she had added to Ken's grief. If he'd told her, if he'd known her well enough, he would have trusted her to understand. The truth had smacked her in the chest. She hadn't understood at all. She'd been shocked. Devastated. Mortified.

While the tidal wave of emotion swallowed her, Annie grasped for her stronghold. Her prayers rolled from her billowing depression. She needed understanding and strength. She prayed for wisdom and compassion. She prayed for Ken...and for herself.

Drawing a deep breath and grasping for hope, Annie started the engine and ventured out on the highway. In a couple of minutes, she pulled into Dee's Café's parking lot and met Jemma extracting Ellie from her car seat.

"Good timing," Jemma said, her smile tender.

With Ellie in one arm, she wrapped the other

around Annie's shoulders as they headed for the door. Inside they found a quiet table and ordered coffee. When the brew arrived, the fragrance sparked life into Annie's spirit. "Hazelnut."

The waitress nodded.

When she'd gone, neither woman drank their coffee. Jemma reached across the table to touch Annie's arm. "This is about Ken."

Surprised, Annie looked into her eyes. "How did you know?"

"Ken talked with Philip a couple days ago."

Annie's pulse tripped as her heart thundered. "Ken talked with Philip about his problems?"

Jemma nodded.

The news stung Annie. He'd talked with Philip and not her.

"Remember when Philip talked about Andrew and how he'd forgiven him? I guess Ken needed to hear how that could be. Somewhere in the conversation he told Philip how much he cared about you, and how he feared telling you about his past, afraid you'd reject him."

Reject him? She'd done that. The other words spread over Annie's heart like a healing balm. "He told Philip that he cared about me?"

"Did you ever question that, Annie? It's as plain as white bread."

Annie grinned. "My vision's blurred, I guess."

"It's natural. People want something so badly they can't believe it when it happens. But Ken has deep feelings for you, Annie. I'd call it love."

*Love.* "If he loved me, why didn't he talk with me, Jemma. Why did he suffer for so long and not let me in? I can't live a life with someone who hides his feelings. Relationships are built on for better or worse." The words settled into her thoughts. *For better or worse.*

"Did you give him a chance?"

"He had months. A year. He never gave me a hint."

"Think about it," Jemma said, "how would you be in the same situation? He'd opened his heart once and had his face slapped. I think anyone would be wary."

"I didn't know about that. Cheryl?"

Jemma nodded. "It's not for me to tell, Annie, but you didn't give Ken a chance to, either."

Annie hadn't. She relived the moment Ken had come to the door. She'd pushed him away. A day earlier she would have known the truth from his lips, not from Susan's. Her sister's behavior knifed her heart. Why? Talk about forgiveness. Susan was a difficult one to forgive.

Annie refocused on Jemma. "You're right. I need to fix that."

"Good for you." Jemma lifted her coffee and took a sip, then grinned. "I think we need a warm-up."

But Annie didn't. Her heart was on fire.

Annie pulled into the driveway, her head filled with her conversation with Jemma. Ken would be home from work soon, and she would call. Apologize. Ask to see him. He cared for her deeply, Jemma had said. That had been her fantasy.

She slid from her car, located the house key on her chain and headed for the porch, her thoughts heavy. Though a mature woman, Annie felt like a girl. Her inexperience settled over her uneasily. She'd never learned the modern rules of romance. Women called men. Women made dates. Women asked men to dance. The boundaries had changed in the past years, and Annie couldn't quite get them reconciled in her mind.

Had she been a modern woman she might have told Ken her feelings long ago. Told him how much she cared about him, loved him. How he'd given her meaning and brought joy to her life. Instead, she'd kept the truth bound in social limitations. She'd rejected him when he needed her the most.

Annie turned the key in the lock and stepped inside. The house smelled dusty. She hadn't cleaned in days. Before she closed the door, a voice called to her and Annie spun around.

Sissy stood behind the screen, holding a container.

Clamping her jaws in place to avoid saying something awful, Annie managed a faint smile. "I'm just getting in from work."

"I was watching for you," Sissy said.

Annie knew that. She pushed open the screen, wishing she could tell Sissy she had no time to talk now. "Come in."

Annie dropped her sweater and purse onto a chair and motioned for Sissy to have a seat. She should be gracious and offer her tea or coffee, but today she couldn't be genial when her life was crumbling at her feet.

When she focused, Sissy had already settled onto the sofa, her back straight, her hands folded in her lap. Something about the look in her eye warned Annie the visit had a deeper purpose than chitchat.

"So what brings you here?" Annie asked, deciding to be direct for a change. She remained standing beside the recliner.

Sissy lifted concerned eyes. "I notice Ken hasn't been by for many days. I hope you aren't having problems."

With her stomach in a knot, Annie paused to find the right words. "We're both fine. Just busy."

Sissy's face wrinkled in a frown. "My niece remembered Ken from Cadillac. Nancy. The one you met."

"Really." She kept her voice noncommital.

"For all his problems, Ken's a wonderful man," Sissy said, her look direct and sincere.

*For all his problems.* Annie clung to her statement. What did Sissy know? "You know about his problems?" Annie asked in as roundabout a way as she could.

Sissy pulled at the collar of her dress. "I hope I haven't said anything wrong."

Annie shifted around the recliner and sank into the cushion. "No. Nothing wrong. I know a little of Ken's problems, but probably not the whole story." Truth won out. She'd hidden her distress long enough.

"It's sad," Sissy said. "He was only a boy. It happened on his eighteenth birthday, Nancy said."

*Eighteenth birthday.* So long ago. The news aroused Annie's desire to learn more. "Breaking and entering. Right?"

Sissy pivoted her head from side to side as if in disbelief. "Yes, but the cottage belonged to the aunt of one of the boys with him. Just four boys celebrating Ken's birthday."

"And they all went to prison?" Annie asked.

"Only Ken. Nancy said the whole thing was so sad. She knew him from school. One boy was put on parole because his family had their priest vouch for him. He was the boy whose aunt owned the cottage."

"And the others?" Annie asked, her heart plummeting against her breastbone.

"Juveniles. They were released on probation." Sissy's face filled with sadness.

"Ken was the only one punished then." The horror of the situation struck Annie. "So unfair."

"Unfair," Sissy repeated. "He was used as an example to other teens, it seems. You know, a small town."

The details loomed in Annie's mind. What he'd been through—his youth, his teen years, and now she'd made things worse.

Eyeing the clock, Annie rose, her thoughts clinging to her need to call Ken. She hoped the action would give Sissy a gentle hint that the visit was ending.

Sissy got her message and rose, her eyes misting as she approached. "Don't let Ken worry that we know about his troubles. I think he'd be much more comfortable keeping it as quiet as possible.'' She made a little cross with her finger over her heart. ''Abby and I both agreed this is one piece of information we'll keep private.''

''Thank you, Sissy. Thank you so much.'' Surprise and appreciation bounded through Annie.

Sissy took a step toward the door, then paused. ''But before I go,'' her face colored to a faint flush, ''I want to tell you something. My own little secret.''

Annie froze in place.

''Don't let Ken's past get in the way of your love, Annie.'' She pressed her papery hand against Annie's arm. ''Years ago I fell in love, but I let my family convince me he was no good for me.'' She blinked her eyes a moment before regaining her calm. ''And then I felt guilty because Abigail was still single. I'm the youngest, you know.''

She lowered her hands and clasped them against her chest. ''I waited too long to accept his proposal. He found someone else.''

Annie's heart plummeted to her toes. ''Oh, Sissy—''

''Days with Edgar were the happiest times of my life, Annie. Don't do what I did. Ken's a good man. Let your heart be your guide.''

''Thank you,'' Annie whispered again, discerning a whiff of lavender as she kissed the woman's cheek.

Sissy gave her a tender smile and hurried to leave.

With moisture brimming her eyes, Annie followed her to the door. When Sissy had left, Annie stood a moment, weighing the woman's words and feeling her sadness.

When she'd controlled her emotions, Annie hurried to the telephone. Ken would be home and they needed to talk. She punched in the numbers and waited.

Disappointed, she heard his answering machine kick in. Electronics was not the way to say what she had to say. She hung up and paced, reliving so many moments and conversations, realizing the sorrow Ken held within himself. Worse than sorrow…fear.

And Cheryl? Had she turned her back on Ken when she heard? Apparently. And how could Annie condemn her? In a way, she'd done the same. She'd pushed him out the door, begging for time to think.

A week had passed. Her thinking had ended. What would her life be without Ken?

Empty.

# *Chapter Nineteen*

Ken threw the last overgrown shrub into the back of his truck and brushed his hands on his pant legs. Tomorrow he would pick up the new ones that Philip had agreed upon along with a mountain ash he'd decided to add to the backyard. Ken had warned him about the berries that would cause his lawn service grief, but Philip didn't care. Jemma wanted the tree with white flowers in early summer and berries just before autumn.

He rounded the house again to gather his tools, but before he made it to the truck, Jemma pulled into the driveway. When she climbed out, she waved, then went about releasing Ellie from the car seat.

When Ellie's feet hit the ground, she headed for Ken. Her round cheeks were as rosy as an apple and her smile as wide as a Halloween pumpkin, with about as many teeth.

"Hi there, beautiful," Ken said, giving the child a wink.

She opened her arms wide and held them toward Ken.

He crouched beside her. "I'm too dirty, Ellie. See my hands." He held up one to show her, but she didn't seem to mind.

Jemma had reached them and moved Ellie out of his way. She studied his face, her smile fading to concern. "How are you?"

He shrugged, not knowing what to say.

"I talked with Annie."

The news triggered a mixture of concern and relief. "How is she?"

"Sorry."

"Sorry?"

Jemma squinted at him in the lowering sunlight. "She cares about you, Ken. She's heartbroken."

"Do you know—"

She nodded. "Husbands and wives often share their concerns. I've kept it to myself, don't worry. And it changes nothing."

He took a deep breath, realizing for the first time in his life he wasn't worried. "It's time I quit living under a dome of fear. I've been ashamed most of my life."

First looking for Ellie's whereabouts, Jemma lifted her hand and rested it on his grit-covered shirt. "You have no call to be ashamed. Your bad days were washed clean the day you acknowledged God's saving grace."

"I'm afraid that wasn't too long ago," he said. "I didn't think sinners belonged in church."

A flicker of a grin came and went from Jemma's face. "If sinners didn't belong there, the church would be empty. We're all sinners. Every one of us."

"I suppose, but mine seemed so much worse."

"Doesn't matter. You've been forgiven, and you have people who care about you. Love you. That's all that matters."

Overwhelmed by the truth, Ken knew he'd let Annie down. He'd witnessed her forgiving heart with her sisters, her father and life itself. Why would he think she wouldn't forgive him? He'd betrayed her friendship.

Jemma gave his arm a squeeze. "Give Annie another chance. Don't run away from her."

*Run away.* He'd run away his entire life.

Today he would stop running.


Dusk had fallen when Ken slipped from his car at Annie's. He reached over the seat and picked up the largest bouquet he'd been able to buy this time of evening. The scent filled the vehicle's interior, reminding him of Annie's sweet perfume.

He clutched the flowers close to his chest, his heart pumping like the old steam engine they'd visited weeks earlier.

Faltering a moment, he stopped on the sidewalk, deciding what to say and envisioning what Annie might do. He'd wrestled with his imagination, asking himself—for better or worse.

For better or worse was all he had to give, and he prayed it was enough for Annie. He looked into the sky, regarding the sliver of moon and knowing that somewhere beyond even dreams God heard his prayer and knew his heart. Annie's faith had unlocked the door for which his mother had tried to give him the key. A key he'd lost for so many years, but found again in the little red book—her New Testament.

Releasing a pent-up breath, Ken took the porch steps slowly, biding for time. When he reached the top, a faint squeak caused him to halt and look to the right. He saw her sitting on the swing.

"You didn't happen to bring your oil can?" Annie's voice murmured through the gloom.

"Sorry. It's in the truck. I could bring it next time."

"That'll work."

She shifted, making space beside her. Ken's spirit lifted as he closed the distance between them. Standing in front of her, he clutched the flowers to his chest.

"Who are the flowers for?"

"The woman I love," Ken said, hearing the words fly from his lips.

"She's a lucky woman."

"I'd say she's blessed," Ken said.

He watched her smile and open her arms. He filled them with the rich bouquet and she buried her nose in its center. "I've never had such a nice present."

"I thought you'd like them," he said.

She leaned over and rested the bouquet on a nearby chair. "I mean you."

Her response caught him off guard. "Me?" He shook his head.

She patted the seat beside her, and Ken lowered his quaking legs into the spot. He slid his arm behind her shoulders and turned her toward him. Without hesitation, his mouth meshed with hers, supple and warm, greeting him with trust and hope.

He drew her closer, feeling her heartbeat against his chest, his own as wild as hers. Deepening the kiss, he heard her soft moan blend with his own. When a warning bell sounded in his head, he calmed his heart and eased back, looking into her eyes with love.

Annie stroked his cheek and rested a finger on the cleft in his chin. "I've been lonely and miserable without you."

"Me, too," he said. "I have so much to explain."

"Not now. We both made mistakes. Mine was not letting you tell me the whole story, but I know most of it, I think."

He gripped her arms and drew back. "The *whole* story?"

She nodded. "And you'll never guess who told me."

"Philip and Jemma?"

"No. Guess again."

His heart hammered. He had no idea. "I can't."

He tilted her head toward Loving Arms. "Sissy and Abby."

Disbelief washed over him. "No."

"Yes."

"How long have they known?"

"Since their niece was here in July. They promised themselves not to say a word." A grin brightened her face. "I'm ashamed at what we said about them."

"Nosy neighbors, but they kept quiet out of Christian love." The reality awed him. "Should I tell you the whole story anyway? I'll feel better."

"For sure, but while you do, please hold me in your arms. I've wanted to be with you like this forever."

"It's a deal—" he brushed his hand along her tied-back hair "—if you'll let down your hair."

She grinned and reached up to unlatch the clip, then pull out the pins. She laid them beside the flowers, then cuddled in his arms.

He held her close, feeling the even beat of her pulse and running his fingers through her hair as he told her everything from the beginning.

Annie never spoke, but her loving tears wetting his shoulder helped to wash away years of anguish. Ken had wanted it to be this way for a lifetime.

Clutching her jacket around her, Annie climbed from the car, her feet crunching in the gravel parking lot. The wind caught in her loosened hair and whipped it across her face. She brushed it away and met Ken coming around the other side.

He laughed, and she knew it was at her impetuous behavior. She'd never let him be a gentleman. She'd been alone too many years. He captured her hand in his and they pushed their feet through the sand and dried leaves scattered by the wind to the long pier.

Ahead of them, the new Loving Light spread its warning to sailors at sea. The old lighthouse stood in darkened silence, still a powerful symbol to Annie. But new or old, the light meant coming home. Since Ken had found his way back to her arms, she'd felt complete and whole—her own kind of homecoming.

The evening they'd talked, she'd cuddled in his arms, her bouquet waiting for water, but her heart drinking in the honest, love-filled confession that Ken shared with her. That day she understood so many things. How Cheryl's hateful rebuff had destroyed his trust and hope. How his parents' rejection conjectured the Lord's abandonment.

But from that moment, life had changed. Ken had opened his wound and allowed her to wash it clean with her love and tears.

"Don't straggle," Ken said, tugging her forward with a grin. "You're the one who wanted to come here."

"I know," she said, not only catching up but shooting past him.

Ken captured her by the waist and spun her around. "I'm not letting you get away from me ever again. This relationship is side by side."

"I like side by side," she said, out of breath, "and I'm too old to be running like a kid."

Ken slipped his arm around Annie's waist and drew her closer. Instead of running, they walked in solid strides to the end of the pier. The wind whipped up the water in foamy waves that splashed against the planks, sending a fine, cold spray over them.

"This is why I wanted to come here," she said.

"To get wet?"

"No, to get renewed."

He arched a brow, his face questioning.

"Look at the water. Churning, seething, wild. Dashing against everything without direction."

"Do I hear something poetic coming on?" Ken asked.

She faced him and clasped his face in her hands. "It's what our lives were. Churning. Going nowhere. No direction or meaning."

From the look in his eyes, she knew he still didn't understand.

"Look up," she said.

He tilted his head as a dashing spray beaded his face. "The lighthouse?"

"The lighthouse," she said, feeling that he'd begun to understand. "Remember? A light to guide us to safety. Calm. Solid. Sure. No matter what mess we're in, in life, the light brings us home."

"God's our lighthouse," he said, his voice confident.

"God and love," she said. "They're the same really. God is love."

They stood a moment, gazes locked, searching, seeking confirmation. She raised herself as high as she could reach, and Ken tilted his face downward, his lips meeting hers, damp with spray and cold from the air, but warm together.

Breathless from the wind's force and Ken's kiss, Annie drew back, savoring the lovely moment.

"I love you," Ken said.

The words lifted Annie higher than the clouds. "I love you heart and soul...and all your loving ways."

Lost in each other's gaze, Annie gasped when a wild wave crashed against the pier and the icy spray covered them in another cold mist. She shivered.

"Had enough?" Ken asked.

"Never."

"Chilly?"

"Not in your arms," she said, trying not to laugh or give way to a shudder.

"How about your fingers?"

Puzzled, she looked at her hands and grinned. "They're fine."

"I had a particular one in mind," he said, sliding his hand into his jacket pocket. "But this might be a dangerous place to give you this gift."

She held her breath, speculating yet disbelieving. When Ken brought out a velvet box and placed it in Annie's hand, she remembered to breathe. She looked down and eyed the cracks between the heavy planks, then looked at Ken, her eyes misted and her heart rejoicing. "I can't wait."

He shrugged. "It's insured."

Annie laughed and cried as she lifted the lid. A diamond glinted in the afternoon sun. A lovely solitaire.

Ken withdrew it from its satin cushion. "Will you marry me, Annie? Please, make my life complete."

"You don't have to ask. Just look in my eyes."

His loving gaze caressed her. "Annie, I know you've worried about having a family, but—"

Touched by his attempt, she shushed him. "I'm forty-three. I don't see children in my future."

Ken's look cautioned her. "I didn't see love in my future, but God had a different idea. Can we leave it in the Lord's hands?"

"It's a deal. The Lord can work miracles...even for an old gal like me."

Ken shook his head. "You're younger than a spring day in my eyes."

With care, he slipped the ring on her finger. The diamond sparkled beside the droplets of lake water sprinkled on her hand. But nothing—diamonds, the lake in sunshine, the Loving Light—nothing shone as sure and steady as God's blessing to them, the gift of love.

\* \* \* \* \*

*If you enjoyed LOVING WAYS, you'll love Gail's next book LOVING CARE, coming in February 2004. Don't miss it!*

Dear Reader,

I hope you enjoyed your third visit to Loving, Michigan. I had so much fun revisiting old friends from the first stories and offering you another look at what's happening in their lives. In 2004, I will make another visit to the resort town on Lake Michigan in a story titled *Loving Care*.

When I began thinking about *Loving Ways,* I wondered what it might be like for people who had devoted their lives to someone's care, then later found themselves without a sense of purpose. Mothers do this when the children have grown. Others do this for ailing and aging parents or sometimes a loving spouse. In *Loving Ways,* Annie learns that God provides strength and comfort to all those who ask for His help…and there's the problem. So often we bear burdens too heavy to carry and forget that two loving arms are reaching out to take our troubles from us. Ken, too, had to learn to trust again and to believe that our loving heavenly Father does not abandon us, but waits for us to call His name.

I pray that each of us stop a moment when we feel abandoned or burdened with problems and remember that the Lord is only waiting for us to ask Him to lift us up and make our burdens light.

*Gail Gaymer Martin*